THAT MUCH SHE KNEW

A murder gets personal for a bold detective

LINDA HAGAN

THE BOOK FOLKS

Published by The Book Folks

London, 2022

This book is a work of fiction. Names, characters, businesses, organizations, places and events are either the product of the author's imagination or are used fictitiously. Any resemblance to actual persons, living or dead, events or locales is entirely coincidental. The spelling is British English.

ISBN 978-1-80462-015-1

www.thebookfolks.com

That Much She Knew is the fifth standalone title by Linda Hagan to feature Belfast detective DCI Gawn Girvin. Details about the other books can be found at the back of this one.

Chapter 1

DCI Gawn Girvin drove carefully down the narrow country lane, trying to prevent the stiletto-sharp hedge scraping the side of her car. Her heart was thumping. Her hands were damp on the steering wheel. She felt sick.

Word had come to her in a brief telephone call from her sergeant. There had been few details. Just enough to set her mind racing. Maxwell, her inspector, was already at the scene but she needed to see for herself.

She had no trouble spotting her destination. The smoke was her guide. Blue-and-white crime scene tape blocked the roadway and was strewn over the hedgerow like streamers abandoned after a boozy Christmas party. Patrol cars were parked haphazardly. Smoke was still rising gently from the exposed rafters of the single-storey dwelling, snaking its way into the sky, and carried onwards on a strengthening breeze.

She had seen two fire engines on her way along the coast road from her home in Carrickfergus past the sleepy little seaside town of Whitehead with its genteel pastel-painted Victorian houses and famous steam railway. Their sirens had been silent. Only a Fire Service car and the rivulets of water cascading down over the tarmac were evidence of their former presence. It was a dreich Tuesday morning, grey, breezy and promising more of the same in the forecast she had listened to with her morning coffee.

She drew her Audi tightly into the side of the lane and glanced at herself in the rear-view mirror. There were dark areas under her eyes. She was not sleeping well again but at least there were no nightmares. Yet. She was still feeling the effects of all the tests she had endured yesterday at hospital. She wasn't allowing herself to think about the implications of any results.

Gawn hooked a stray wisp of hair behind her ear, pulled a waterproof hat down firmly on her head, stepped out of the car and braced herself against the wind and rain. Then she stood. Still. She was taking in the whole scene – the sights, the sounds, the smells. Less than twelve hours earlier she had stood on almost the same spot and waved goodbye to Harriet Hughes. Now Harriet was dead. Murdered.

Chapter 2

Inspector Paul Maxwell approached his boss. His face showed he hadn't expected to see her.

His coat collar was pulled up offering some protection from the wind but his hair was already wet, plastered tightly to his forehead. Beads of rain were running down his cheeks and he looked cold.

He had seen the DCI arriving and quickly finished his conversation with the Fire Service's area deputy commander before walking over to speak to her. He didn't need to rush. She would use these first minutes to get a feel for the crime scene. That was what she always did. But by the time Maxwell reached her, she was preparing for action, leaning back against her car, exchanging her latest Jimmy Choos for a pair of green wellies. Her heavy gabardine coat and hat, so suitable for the weather this morning, made her look like a model readying herself for some photoshoot for stylish rainwear.

'Good morning, ma'am.'

He managed a weak smile in spite of the cold and damp and the trickle of rain making its way down his neck under his shirt collar. He stamped his feet to try to get some heat back into them.

'Is it?'

Her voice was dull and lifeless as if she was fed up or even in shock, like a witness rather than an experienced police officer who had been in situations just like this a hundred times before.

She saw his look of surprise at her response and realised her tone of voice had betrayed how she was feeling. She knew she'd been looking tired recently too. Hardly surprising.

'Well, obviously not for our vic,' Maxwell agreed.

'So, what do we know so far?'

Her eyes were scanning all around as she spoke, not looking directly at him. It was almost as if there was something or someone she was expecting to see but who wasn't there. She was tense, even more tense than was usual at the start of a case.

Straight down to business. The Ice Queen, they called her. She knew that was her nickname. She put up barriers around herself, not seeking popularity, but there were chinks in her icy armour. Just very occasionally she couldn't manage to hide a layer of vulnerability from the world.

But she was dedicated to her work – sometimes too much, she knew – and she expected that same commitment from everyone on her team. She was hard to live up to. And she knew she sometimes took chances to get results. She had the highest clear-up rate in the Police Service of Northern Ireland and that caused some jealousy among her colleagues. But she didn't care. Results were all that mattered to her.

'Our vic's Harriet Hughes. She's in her early forties, we think.'

'You don't know how old she is?' Gawn interrupted him, her left eyebrow lifting in the quizzical expression he knew so well.

'Not yet, boss. Give us a chance. The locals took their time calling us in. They thought they were dealing with an accidental death, someone falling running away to escape the fire.'

A year ago he wouldn't have dared to speak to her like that but, ever since the sexual abuse case that none of them would ever forget, their relationship had changed. She knew he admired her but he didn't follow her unquestioningly as he once had.

'We can't get into the house yet to look for any personal documents. The Fire Service has just given the all-clear, but the CSIs will keep us out until they've finished. Anyhow, according to one of the neighbours, Mrs Hughes was Scottish, he thinks, or maybe English but not local anyway. We're working on finding out more about her but her age is low priority. No matter what age she was, she's dead now.'

This last comment had sounded harsh and Gawn realised just how fed up he must be. He was the one who had been standing out in the rain from the early hours of the morning trying to piece together exactly what had happened. Now she had arrived and wanted all the answers ready for her. He paused, no doubt expecting a reaction from her, she realised, but when she didn't respond, he continued.

'She was a teacher in a special school until just a couple of weeks ago and then she just left. Again, this is all according to the neighbour so we'll need to check it out for ourselves. She was an artist or was trying to be one anyway.' Maxwell's voice showed what he thought of that. 'She'd lived here, in this rented bungalow, for about six weeks. The doc says death was probably due to blunt force trauma to the back of the skull but you know what they're like. I was lucky to get that. Anyway, I could see the wound on the back of her head for myself.'

'Did you get a preliminary time of death?' Gawn asked.

'Some time before midnight, probably between eight and twelve.'

She was glad he was watching some of the CSIs at work so he hadn't seen her reaction to his words.

'Then whoever attacked her tried to set fire to the house. Lucky for us, they weren't too successful. The fire brigades put it out quite quickly.'

'Who found her?'

'Her husband.'

'Her husband?' Gawn's voice was raised in surprise.

'You mean her *estranged* husband?' she said.

'You know her, I mean, you knew her, ma'am?'

Now his face registered surprise. The DCI liked to keep her private life very much to herself. She seldom socialised with anyone from the job. There was no good reason why she shouldn't have known Harriet Hughes. She collected works of art. Perhaps that was how the two women had met.

'Not very well. I'd only seen her a couple of times.'

'Recently?'

Reluctantly she said, 'Last night.'

Maxwell looked stunned by her answer.

'You met her somewhere last night?' he repeated carefully.

'No. I was *here* last night, Paul. They'll be able to match my car tracks. I was stopped just up in front of the house there. I knocked but no one answered so I thought she wasn't home. I was just about to drive off when I saw her at the front window. She saw me but she obviously didn't want to speak to anyone so I left.' Then a thought seemed to strike her. 'Who pronounced her?'

'Munroe. Why?' he asked.

'Not Norris?'

Jenny Norris was Gawn's friend and Professor Al Munroe's number two in the Forensic Pathology Department. The two enjoyed a constant tussle. They respected each other's work but they were very different characters. Munroe was older, set in his ways, meticulous to the point of being pernickety. His attitudes and his old-fashioned dress sense and expanding waistline, coupled with an ever-decreasing amount of hair on his head, gave him an almost Dickensian appearance. It led to his being a target, behind his back of course, for the jokes of many of his colleagues. His expertise was respected but he was not particularly well liked.

Jenny Norris was not only younger and easier on the eye but her years spent working in Boston meant she was keen to try every new technique and trend in forensic pathology. She was chatty and outgoing and had fitted in easily since moving back to Belfast while Munroe was on sabbatical. The chief pathologist didn't respond to many call-outs himself these days. Gawn was glad he had this time.

'Someone will have to let her know.' She hesitated for a moment. 'I'll do it.'

'Why does Jenny need to know? Munroe was going to do the PM himself this afternoon, I think. You don't want Jenny to do it, do you?'

'God, no. Definitely not.' Gawn's voice was forced.

A spark of understanding showed on Maxwell's face.

'Were they close friends?'

Jenny Norris made no secret of the fact she was gay.

Before the DCI had time to add anything else, a black van drew almost silently past them, its electric motor inaudible but its wheels crunching on the tarmac. One of the police cars was being moved to let it pass.

'I think Munroe intended doing the PM this afternoon. That's what he said anyway when he was leaving,' Maxwell said.

'Then I'd better phone Dr Norris now. I don't want her seeing the victim arriving in a body bag. She'll need to have time to prepare herself.'

'I don't think she's at the mortuary.'

'I didn't think it was her day off.'

In fact she knew it wasn't. Jenny Norris had already spent her day off yesterday with her.

'It isn't,' Maxwell said. 'Munroe was complaining he'd had to come himself because she hadn't turned up for work this morning and hadn't even phoned in to explain why. He was having a good old moan about it. You can imagine what he was like. You know how he always likes to find something to criticise her for.'

It wasn't like Jenny to miss work or even to be late. And not even bothering to explain why. That didn't sound like her friend at all. Jenny was highly professional, and Gawn couldn't see her just skiving off for the day, but she could understand why she might have needed a bit of time off. Gawn knew Jenny and the victim had had a row last night. She remembered how upset Jenny had been when she had phoned and asked her to visit Harriet and try to talk some sense into her. Jenny had been so worried about her friend.

'I'll try calling her now, Paul. Maybe she's not feeling well. If she's at home, I'll arrange to go over and see her after I've finished here. I don't want to break the news to her over the phone, especially if she's already feeling under the weather. You go ahead. I'll catch you up.'

She watched his forlorn figure trudging up the slight incline towards the bungalow, hands pushed down deep into his pockets trying to keep them warm, shoulders slightly hunched. The rain was starting to come down even harder now. Gawn could feel it bouncing off her Drizabone coat and being driven into her face like a fusillade of tiny sharp needles.

She listened impatiently for the call to connect. It began to ring and then she realised she could hear a phone ringing somewhere nearby. She recognised the ringtone – *Hail to the Chief* – Jenny's little joke. She started searching around following the sound until she spotted the mobile lying tight under the hedge, just at the edge of the outer cordon.

'Bring a marker and an evidence bag over here. I need this photographed and then bagged,' she shouted to the nearest white-clad figure. 'And move this cordon further out.'

She watched while her orders were carried out. All the time questions were forming in her mind. What was Jenny's phone doing here? Exactly when had she been here to leave it behind? And, most urgently, where was she now if her phone was here?

One woman was dead and another missing, it seemed. She needed answers. And she needed them as soon as possible and preferably before anyone else knew about Jenny's connection to Harriet Hughes.

Chapter 3

'This was the seat of the fire.'

Maxwell was reporting what he'd been told. He was pointing to a badly burned section in the hallway. They knew better than to set foot inside the building before the CSIs gave them the all-clear. Gawn seemed to be only half-listening. Something was troubling her but she didn't say anything so he ignored it.

Maxwell's voice droned on.

'They'll have to do more tests but the deputy commander seemed pretty definite that it was a half-hearted attempt to burn the place down. Just some papers and some cloth. He thought it was probably some old tea towels from the scraps they found and a drop of petrol and matches. Simple as that. Our arsonists wouldn't have had to bring anything special with them. He suggested it probably wasn't premeditated, just a spur of the moment thing to cover their tracks.'

'Remind me when we seconded him to the Serious Crimes Squad, Paul,' Gawn responded sarcastically. 'I don't go around telling him how to do his job and we don't need any helpful suggestions from outsiders about the motivation of our perp. We'll do it the old-fashioned way and find evidence.'

'Right, boss.'

It had been a long time since she had sounded so snarky. Maxwell would think she had got out of the wrong side of the bed this morning. Or maybe she was ill or she and Seb, her husband, had had a row or were splitting up.

'Whoever did it and whatever they used, I think he's probably right,' she reluctantly conceded. 'It was probably an attempt to cover their tracks. It's too coincidental otherwise. My money's on Mr Hughes. All we have to do now is find the evidence.'

'You seem pretty sure Hughes is our perp. Couldn't it just have been a burglary gone wrong? Mrs Hughes could have disturbed someone breaking in and they panicked and hit her.'

Maxwell was trying to suggest alternatives. Gawn knew he would think she was jumping to conclusions. Just because the man had found the body didn't mean he'd killed his wife, even if they were estranged. She knew that but she tried to justify her attitude to him.

'He's the most likely candidate, isn't he? At the very least he's a person of interest.'

'Why would Hughes want to burn the place down?' Maxwell asked. 'If he was inside the property, he had a perfect reason for being there. He was married to the woman. He wouldn't have had to try to hide being inside.'

'Maybe he wanted to get us to think someone else had been here and was trying to destroy evidence.'

It sounded like she was trying to convince him and maybe herself too that Hughes was the killer.

'Would Hughes have had the presence of mind to think out how to throw the blame on to someone else? That sounds more like the plot of one of those psychological detective dramas on the telly. Far-fetched,' Maxwell argued, scrunching up his face to show what he thought of her suggestion. They both knew most criminals weren't that clever or that cunning when planning their murders, especially when it came to domestic violence.

'But he hadn't just killed her, Paul, had he? You said TOD was before midnight. What time did he call the Fire Service?'

'The call came in just after seven this morning.'

'So he had all night to think about it. And did our friendly fireman give you any indication of how long the fire had been burning? It didn't burn the place down so it can't have been burning all night.'

'He talked about it smouldering,' Maxwell said, 'but they'd have to do tests before he could be more definite.'

'Anyhow, with luck, there should be something for Forensics to find. They should be able to turn up some hard evidence of who was here – Hughes or anyone else – and whoever set the fire. Let's leave it to them for now,' she concluded, bringing their speculation to an end.

Chapter 4

Even from outside the smell of petrol, mingled with the smell of charred wood, melted plastic and smoke, was catching at their throats. The walls in the hallway were blackened, the once dainty floral print wallpaper showing through only in patches like a pretty pink rash. The central light fitting was hanging at a crazy angle, its plastic cover melted into a Daliesque creation where the fire had burned up the wall and flashed across the ceiling, eating up into the roof space above and setting fire to the rafters.

'You're right, boss. It doesn't look like it got much of a chance to really get going, does it? If it had been burning all night, you'd think there would be nothing left. But if it wasn't Hughes and it hadn't been smouldering all night, then he must have arrived very soon after it was lit. That means our perp must have hung around after the murder. Maybe he was looking for something and had just found it or he'd given up before the husband arrived. Or maybe Hughes arrived and scared him off when he spotted the fire and phoned it in and then found his wife.'

Gawn reacted to what Maxwell had just said.

'He didn't look for his wife first?'

'I don't know. I only had a chance for a quick word with him. He didn't say but she wasn't inside the house. Her body was found up the lane.'

'But when he found the place on fire, he didn't know she wasn't inside, did he, Paul? What would your first reaction be if you came across your house on fire?'

'I know what you're getting at, boss. I would run in and see if Kerri and the kids were there. But, if Hughes and his wife were estranged, then this wasn't his house and he probably didn't have a key. And he might just have assumed she wasn't at home.'

'Where would she be likely to be at seven o'clock in the morning?' she asked sharply. 'And would any of that have stopped you? You'd have wanted to be sure. And why was he even here so early? Funny sort of time to go visiting. What was he doing here?'

'I don't know anything about any of that, boss. He didn't mention anything about living apart. I just kind of assumed they were together and he'd just arrived home, maybe after a night shift or something.'

The DCI looked at Maxwell sternly. She had warned him often enough about assuming things. Yet, wasn't that what she was doing too? From what she had heard of him, Hughes was capable of violence and she realised she wanted it to be him. She wanted a nice quick resolution, an arrest, a case closed. Neat and tidy. Present it all to Superintendent McDowell with no questions about Jenny and the victim.

'Where's Hughes now?' Gawn asked.

'He was a bit shook up. One of the neighbours took him in and they're giving him a cup of tea. I sent a PC across with him to keep an eye, just in case.'

He didn't elaborate. Gawn could see he was puzzled by her attitude to the victim's husband. She knew she was coming across as too adamant he was their killer without the evidence to back it up.

Just then Gawn's attention was attracted by the whirring of a drone which one of the CSIs was using to take some aerial photographs of the scene. She had half-turned to watch the mechanical insect rise into the sky when she became aware of someone walking across behind her. She swung round.

'Lyons,' she called out.

Damien Lyons halted in his tracks. Knowing her reputation, she thought he would have hoped to get past without attracting her attention.

'Yes, ma'am.'

'Is Mark Ferguson not on duty today?'

She preferred to have Mark Ferguson as her crime scene manager when she could. She knew him and she knew his work. He was meticulous. Damien Lyons was young. She didn't know him well and she hadn't been able to form any opinion yet of his work. She liked quick results but she liked careful work too. Ferguson managed that balance. She didn't want some new man trying to impress her, rushing to get answers and missing something.

'He's giving evidence in court this morning, ma'am. I'm supervising this one.'

He sounded nervous and Gawn knew she could be intimidating. She didn't always mean to be but sometimes it was a useful way to get results quickly.

'What have you got so far?'

Gawn knew the young officer would probably like to tell her it was early days yet; he'd hardly had a chance to get started. She knew Mark Ferguson would be training him to stand up for himself. She could just imagine his advice to Lyons, 'Don't take any shit from any of them, Damien. You're the boss until you give them the word. It's your crime scene.'

Instead, Lyons replied, 'We have the victim's car parked over there and her husband's vehicle was here too. Then there are three other sets of tyre tracks. The vehicles must have been here recently. Probably within the last twelve to twenty-four hours. We've preserved the tread marks and we should be able to identify the type and if we get a suspect vehicle, we'll be able to match them.'

'Start with my car. I was here very briefly last night. I drove up to the front of the house, did a three-point turn and left again.'

'Yes, ma'am.' If he was shocked at her admission, he managed to mask it.

'Then you can concentrate on the other sets.'

'Yes, ma'am.' She thought he would have agreed to anything to get away.

'What about inside the house?'

'We haven't been inside yet, ma'am. We started on the area around the body. We couldn't get inside until we got the all-clear that it was safe. A second team will begin working inside now.'

The mortuary van made its way slowly past them heading back to the main road as the trio stood at the front door. Gawn noticed the young CSI bow his head slightly as it passed. She had no problem with that. She always insisted anyone working on her cases showed respect to the victims no matter what condition their body might be in or who they were.

'Can you clear me to see where our victim was attacked?' Gawn asked.

'We're not sure yet exactly where that was, Chief Inspector.'

No doubt expecting a curt response Lyons hurried on trying to explain himself.

'I mean, we've identified and begun processing the area around where the body was found, and you can certainly see that, but they've taken the body away now. Inspector Maxwell gave the all-clear to move it. There won't be much left to see. The pathologist will need to say whether that was where the attack took place or if her body was moved.'

She looked a little embarrassed and said, 'You're quite right. I made an assumption.'

She looked across at Maxwell and, for the first time this morning, smiled at him. 'She could have been attacked inside the house or somewhere else and tried to run away. But there's no point in guessing. I'll leave it up to you to establish the facts and I'll await your report… as soon as possible.'

'Of course, Chief Inspector.'

He turned and hurried past them into the house, glad to get away from the Ice Queen before she thought of any more awkward questions.

Gawn watched him go.

'He has the makings of a good CSM,' she said.

'He kept you on your toes anyway.' And Maxwell smirked.

Chapter 5

Maxwell accompanied Gawn back to her car and sat alongside her as she exchanged her heavy boots, now wet and muddy, for more fashionable footwear. He seemed to be working himself up to saying something.

Eventually he blurted out, 'Don't you think you should step aside from the investigation? After all, you had a personal relationship with the victim and you were here last night.'

Her hand paused for just a second and then she continued pulling her boot off as if he hadn't spoken. She didn't rush to respond. She had had a case before which had involved her then boyfriend, now husband, Sebastian York and it had proved tricky for her. The criminals had been able to use his part in it all, innocent as it was, against her and she had had to face up to some moral challenges about how far she would go to protect him.

'I didn't have a personal relationship with Harriet Hughes, Paul. I met her once. And, yes, I was here last night. Jenny asked me to come and talk to her but, as I've already explained to you, when she didn't open the door, I just waved at her and drove off again. Nothing more. I think I can be objective. In fact, I know I can. There's no conflict of interest.'

Maxwell's face showed he didn't believe her. She was being too adamant and her earlier reactions had made him suspicious. He sensed she was hiding something although he couldn't think what. And he thought she didn't really believe what she'd just said herself. Jenny Norris was obviously involved in some way and the fact that she'd asked Gawn to come and talk to the victim last night was bound to come out eventually. He just hoped Hughes would confess to attacking his wife. He could plead manslaughter. He hadn't meant to kill her. It had been an accident. Then they could close it all up quickly before anything about Jenny's and the DCI's involvement with the victim came to light.

There was a pause again and Maxwell wondered what she was going to say next. She was going to drop some bombshell. He knew her well enough to know that.

'I found Jenny's phone.'

'When? Where?'

'When I was trying to ring her. I heard it ringing over there. You can see where they marked its position before they moved it.' She pointed to the yellow marker under the hedge.

'So she was here last night too.'

'I already knew she'd been here. Well, actually I didn't.' She contradicted herself. 'I knew she'd had a row with Harriet. I kind of just assumed it had been on the phone.' She had the good grace to look embarrassed as she admitted that. 'Anyway, she phoned me after the argument. She sounded a bit upset and she asked me to come and talk to Harriet. So that's why I was here.'

'She'd had a row with the victim last night? She was upset when she phoned you? When was this?'

Gawn felt like a suspect being questioned.

'Around nine o'clock or a little later.'

Although it had still been early, Gawn had already been dressed in one of Seb's old T-shirts that she liked to sleep in. She'd been physically and mentally exhausted after her day at the hospital and had planned to take a couple of sleeping tablets and head to bed, hopeful of getting a better night's sleep. She had told Jenny she would phone Harriet Hughes and speak to her but her friend had pleaded that she go and talk to her in person. Carrickfergus wasn't far away, she'd argued. It was only a few minutes' drive. Eventually Gawn had given in.

'So she must have dropped her phone here in a rush to get away before you arrived,' Maxwell said. Gawn could almost hear the barrister's closing argument to the jury.

'We don't know if she was here when she phoned me. She could have phoned me from home. That's where I thought she was. And anyway Harriet was alive then, remember? I saw her. And even if Jenny did come back later, she might not have got in, the same as me.'

Gawn's voice trailed off as she realised the implications of what she was saying.

'She could just have lost it out of her pocket or something. She wasn't necessarily running away. Harriet probably wouldn't have let her in either. You can't think she phoned me and then came back after I'd been here to kill Harriet.'

Maxwell's response was immediate. 'I don't know what to think other than this is going to get bloody messy. Don't you think it would be better if you let me take over or you'll just get tangled up in it?' he pleaded.

In fact she already was, whether she realised it or not. But she was an intelligent woman. Of course, she realised it. But Maxwell knew how bloody-minded she could be.

She spoke quietly but very firmly, a voice that implied she would brook no contradiction.

'I know you'd do a good job, Paul. This is not about you. It's about me. I'm already tangled up in this whether I like it or not. I know that. And I know it won't be easy. But I can do my job. I can follow the evidence and be objective.'

But even as she was speaking, she realised herself that if Jenny Norris was involved in this in some way, it would be much harder for her to remain objective. And her friendship with the pathologist could be used against both of them.

But she had made her mind up. She wouldn't be talked out of it. She knew Maxwell could go over her head to Superintendent McDowell and report her involvement with the victim, and a possible suspect. He could have her taken off the case but she hoped he wasn't going to do that. She would never forgive him and she'd never trust him again if he did. She hoped he knew her well enough by now to have her back and try to make sure she didn't do anything stupid, anything which might compromise the case or her own career.

Gawn was relieved when Maxwell spoke again. It seemed he was going to go along with her, at least for now.

'Why were you here last night, boss? What did Jenny tell you?'

'I've already told you, Paul. She phoned me and asked me to come. Harriet Hughes had left her husband a few weeks ago. He was abusive, sometimes violent and he was still giving her a hard time. Jenny had tried to talk to her about what she should do. She'd suggested getting a restraining order against him but they'd had an argument so she wanted me to have a go at talking to her and give her some advice.'

'They'd had an argument?' He enunciated slowly, letting unspoken ideas hang in the air between them.

'Yes. OK. I know what you're thinking, Paul, but they were just friends. Nothing more.'

'And you know this, how?'

'OK. I know because that's what Jenny told me. So you're going to suggest that she could have been lying to me, that she was hiding the fact they were in some kind of a relationship and she came here and they had another row. And then what? She decided to get me involved too? She was devious enough to plan ahead and think about how she could use me to subvert the investigation so she could get away with murder? Come on, Paul. Does that sound like Jenny to you?'

Her voice had risen slightly as she spoke. Even to her ears, it sounded like an unlikely but possible hypothesis to argue. If she didn't know Jenny, if this was just a case she was coming to cold, it was probable that she would have suspected her.

'Knowing Jenny, it doesn't seem likely that she would cold-bloodedly kill somebody and be devious enough to involve you but then not everyone knows Jenny. We need to find her, and hear what really happened,' Maxwell argued.

'We've got her phone. We should be able to get information about her calls and where she was when they were made. It'll tell us if she was here when she made the call to me.'

'But she left the phone behind. That could have been to stop us tracking her through it, couldn't it?'

'Now you sound as if she's a suspect, Paul.'

'Well, she has to be, doesn't she?' He didn't add that she could end up as a suspect too but he thought it.

She looked at him. She could see he wasn't happy to think of the pathologist in this way either. Reluctantly, she agreed.

'But once we find her, she'll explain how her phone came to be here and what happened last night. In the meantime let's have a word with the husband. He's still the frontrunner for me.'

Chapter 6

The neighbouring bungalow, belonging to an elderly couple called the Binghams, looked almost exactly the same as the one they had just left. Both were little, white-washed boxes with glossy red front doors and planting containers on their windowsills, the colourful flowers gone leaving only sad greenery struggling to avoid the hardships of the coming winter. The two houses had been built on adjoining parcels of farmland by someone hoping to raise some cash developing their no-longer-needed arable pasture. Identical layouts taken from a book of bungalow plans and the cheapest self-build materials had resulted in the construction of mirrored dwellings.

Maxwell knocked, then stood back and waited. A tall elderly gentleman dressed in dark brown corduroy trousers which didn't quite reach his ankles revealing a flash of garish pink socks opened it. He looked down at them over his spectacles which were perched precariously on the end of a rather bulbous nose. He had the look of an owlish academic but his voice, when he spoke, had a surprisingly strong country accent.

'Can I help you?'

'DCI Girvin and DI Maxwell.' Gawn held up her ID. 'Mr Hughes is here, I believe. We'd like a word with him.'

'Come in, officers.'

The householder stepped back and let them walk past him into the hallway. Gawn noticed it was decorated in the same pink flowery wallpaper she had seen in patches on the wall of the burned hallway.

'He's in here.'

The man half-shuffled along in front of them leading the way. He opened a door to reveal a small living room where a man and a woman were sitting talking, their backs to the incomers. Gawn took in the scene. Every available surface seemed to be covered with ornaments and framed family photographs. A fire was blazing up the chimney and a wave of welcoming heat hit them. The woman was leaning across between the two armchairs, patting the man on the arm in a gesture of sympathy. She looked round when they entered. Her look was quizzical and slightly belligerent, as if she were annoyed at the interruption.

'Here's two police officers, love. They want to speak to Mr Hughes,' the homeowner explained.

'*Doctor* Hughes,' the seated man corrected him without turning, his voice sounding waspish.

Gawn was reminded of her first ever meeting with Sebastian York when he had insisted on the use of his title of 'Doctor'. She had not been impressed then and she was not impressed now.

Hughes stood up slowly and turned around to face them before speaking again. She had heard plenty about him from Jenny when they'd had dinner together at the weekend and then again yesterday when they had waited together at the hospital, but this was the first time she had seen him.

She thought he looked more annoyed than upset. But she was surprised at just how ordinary he looked. She supposed she'd built up her own image of what he would look like from what she had been told about him. But there was nothing about Edward Hughes to make him stand out in a crowd; nothing to suggest he could be violent or dangerous. Rather the opposite. He looked rather timid with his wire-rimmed spectacles and a thin moustache reminiscent of the attempts of spotty adolescents to look more macho. But Gawn had met many murderers who were small, ineffectual-looking characters whose physical appearance belied the awful things they had done.

The man standing facing her now was slightly built. His dark wavy hair was unruly and she had already recognised his mannerism of running his hand through it to try to keep it back off his face. She glanced at his shoes and saw they were wet, like Maxwell's. The legs of his jeans were wet too and the knees were muddy. He was wearing a pale blue shirt and Gawn wondered where his coat was. Surely he'd been wearing a coat on a cold wet morning like today. His skin was pale, almost translucent but she thought it was more likely his natural complexion rather than the effects of shock, and his eyes were red-ringed from crying.

'Dr Hughes, we're sorry for your loss. I appreciate you've had a terrible shock but in cases like these we need to get started looking for whoever did this to your wife as quickly as possible. The more time passes, the more likely they are to get away so we'd really appreciate it if you could try to answer some questions for us.'

Gawn put as much sympathy into her voice as she could muster. She must not jump to conclusions, she reminded herself sternly. Easier said than done. She so wanted it to be this man but she would take it carefully. If they could get him talking, he might incriminate himself. Perhaps it had been a moment of anger and he would be glad to confess, to get it off his conscience.

Gawn already knew from what Jenny Norris had told her that Hughes was capable of acts of violence towards his wife but he was always remorseful afterwards. He lost his temper and perhaps that was what had happened here.

'Jenny had told her.' The phrase rang through her mind. Had Jenny been lying to her? Or at least not telling her everything? How much of what she thought she knew about this man and his marriage had Jenny told her and she had just accepted? They would have to start from scratch, find out everything for themselves, check and double-check.

'I'll leave you to it then.' The woman stood up, reluctantly it seemed. She took a now empty cup from Hughes' hand where he was still clutching it, like a mother taking a mug from a baby, put her hand briefly on his shoulder and then walked out of the room giving the two police officers a hostile glance as she walked past.

'Thank you, Daphne, for your kindness,' Hughes called after her. He seemed stunned but that was hardly surprising.

Uninvited, Gawn took the seat the woman had just vacated. Hughes flopped down again in the armchair beside her as if his legs had suddenly lost all power. They had arranged on the way over that Gawn would interview Hughes. Maxwell would merely observe.

'Who are you again?' Hughes asked almost in a daze, his face crumpling in an effort to understand or remember what he had been told. He looked directly at her as he asked the question and scanned her face as if the answer would be written there.

'I'm Detective Chief Inspector Gawn Girvin and this is Detective Inspector Paul Maxwell. We're from the Serious Crimes Squad, sir.'

Hughes nodded as if satisfied that they were appropriate people to be investigating his wife's murder.

'Do I know you? Your name's familiar.' He wrinkled his brow and studied her face closely as if trying to remember.

'No. We've never met. You've had a shock, sir, but maybe you could try to take us through exactly what happened this morning.'

Hughes seemed to be gathering his thoughts. He folded his hands in his lap and sat back in the chair, half-closing his eyes as if trying to visualise for himself what had happened. Gawn noticed his hands were shaking slightly. Perhaps he really was in shock. Perhaps her judgement of him had been harsh. Or perhaps he was nervous about having to answer their questions, fearing discovery of his guilt.

'I was driving up the lane when I saw the smoke.'

'The house was already on fire when you arrived?'

'Yes. Of course.' His brow wrinkled in consternation.

'Did you go inside?'

'No. I tried to. I banged on the door but it was locked. I tried to break in but it's not like in the movies, is it?'

He half-smiled at his own question.

'I only managed to hurt my shoulder.' He rubbed at his left shoulder tentatively as if to verify his account. 'The door wouldn't budge,' he said.

'Then what did you do?'

'I phoned 999. I knew they would be able to break it down.'

'Did you try to get in around the back of the building?'

'No.'

'Or consider breaking a window to get in?'

As if he realised his admissions were putting him in a bad light, he said, 'I… I… was panicking. I wasn't thinking logically. I think I remembered that I'd read somewhere or that I'd heard from someone that you shouldn't give fire any oxygen. I thought if I broke a window it might actually make it worse.'

'So you just stood and watched it burn and waited?'

Gawn couldn't help a touch of cynicism sounding in her voice. Really? He had just stood outside and waited while his wife might be burning to death inside? They might have been estranged but surely he'd had some feelings left for her, especially if he was trying to convince her to give their marriage another go? You would try to rescue a total stranger, never mind someone you loved, wouldn't you?

Hughes was fidgeting. He couldn't seem to keep his hands or legs still. Gawn imagined he looked like someone suffering from St Vitus' Dance. Not that she knew what that looked like. There was even a twitch to the side of his eye.

'It sounds awful when you put it like that but yes, I suppose so. They were very quick. I think. I mean it all seemed so fast and so slow all at the same time. And unreal. Like it wasn't really happening. It was like a dream. A nightmare.'

He started to weep then, taking off his glasses and wiping his tears away with the back of his hand.

Gawn waited a moment to let him compose himself.

'So how did you come to find your wife then, sir?'

He seemed to pull himself together and stood up before he answered. He began pacing quickly up and down in front of the fire, tapping his hand on his leg in time with his agitated steps as if he couldn't stay still any longer. The room was small and he didn't have much space. He was almost knocking against Gawn's knees every time he passed across in front of her. He was like a lion pacing in a cage at the zoo. Abruptly, he stopped, swung round to face her and looked directly into her eyes. Just at that moment coals in the fire behind him collapsed, sending a shower of sparks up the chimney, the noise breaking the moment of silence.

'They moved me back. The firemen. When they came. They needed to get in to search for Harriet and get their equipment inside and I was in the way, they said. They told me to wait in my car. But I didn't want to go back down the hill.' Now his words were coming in a rush.

'You were parked near the bottom of the lane, sir?' Maxwell asked.

He knew he wasn't supposed to ask anything. That was the arrangement they had made. Gawn threw him an annoyed look. She didn't want Hughes to be interrupted. He was talking. That was good. They needed to keep him talking. The more he talked, the more likely he was to make a mistake.

'Yes. I stopped and jumped out as soon as I saw the smoke and ran up to the door.'

'So where did you go then, Dr Hughes, when the firemen sent you away?' Gawn asked.

'I went up the loanen towards the back field.'

Gawn noted that Hughes seemed to be familiar with the layout of the bungalow and the area even though he hadn't been living here.

'I don't know what I was thinking; where I thought I was going.'

His hand went to his hair again and flicked it back out of his eyes in that same mannerism Gawn had already noted.

'Maybe I had some idea of coming over here to tell them in case they'd seen the smoke but I don't know. I… I… I was confused. And then I saw her. Harriet. Lying there. Just lying in the middle of the loanen.'

A sob caught his voice. He stopped moving and stopped speaking. Gawn could see tears forming in his eyes again. He started to rock back and forth as she had seen men do at the Wailing Wall on a visit to Jerusalem.

'I saw her body just lying there… and her head and all the blood.'

He put both his hands up to his mouth as if trying to hold in any more words.

'Did you touch your wife, sir?' Maxwell asked.

Hughes glanced down at his hands, turning them over to look at the backs before he answered.

'Of course I touched her.'

He turned an angry look on the inspector.

'I wanted to see how badly hurt she was. I wanted to hold her, to comfort her. I don't think I realised she was dead. Not straight away. Maybe I did but my mind just wouldn't accept it. Then I saw the blood all over my hands and my coat and I knew then.'

He stopped talking abruptly and, as if he had deflated like a pricked balloon, slumped back down into the chair. He started to cry unashamedly, burying his face in his hands. Gawn remembered how Jenny had told her he often cried when asking Harriet for forgiveness after he had given her another set of bruises or a black eye.

'You've washed your hands, sir?' she asked.

'Yes. Of course. I couldn't look at all the blood on them. Her blood.'

'And where's your coat, Dr Hughes?' Gawn was looking around the room but there was no sign of it.

'Daphne took it to try to clean it up a bit for me.'

Gawn didn't need to say anything. The expression she cast towards the constable said it all. Maxwell was already on his way to the door to retrieve the coat, taking the PC with him to get him out of her way.

Gawn would have liked to continue the questioning but just then the door swung open and a woman she didn't recognise rushed in, almost colliding with Maxwell on his way out. She ignored the two men and knelt down in front of Hughes, totally ignoring Gawn too. She drew his head into her body and hugged him.

'I'm so sorry, Edward. It's so awful about poor Harriet and you finding her. It must have been such a shock for you.'

Then she seemed to notice Gawn as if for the first time. She looked up at her, then moved back slightly from Hughes and took his hand and patted it tenderly.

'Thank you for coming so quickly, Nats.' Hughes looked at her and tried a weak smile through his tears.

'I came as soon as I could, Eddie. Mum phoned me but I was in a meeting with a client. I got here just as soon as I could.'

Gawn didn't want to let the interview get away from her.

'Sorry. You are?'

'I'm Natalie Bingham. This is my parents' house. Edward and I are old friends.'

She said this as if she expected her name to mean something to the policewoman.

'We've met before.' She was looking past Gawn and speaking to Maxwell who had just come back into the room.

He was shaking his head. Gawn was surprised he didn't remember her. He usually had an eye for an attractive woman and Natalie Bingham certainly was that.

'The Falloon case. I was representing Nicholas Hunter. We met at a consultation in the High Court.'

A look of realisation came over Maxwell's face.

'Yes. Ms Bingham. You were briefed by Hartnett & Magill. I remember now, of course.'

Another one who liked everyone to know who they were and treat her accordingly. Gawn would not be treating Natalie Bingham deferentially just because she was a QC. She didn't believe in any special treatment for anyone who stood in the way of her investigation, whoever they were. She had a murderer to find. And quickly.

Chapter 7

Natalie Bingham put an end to their questions.

'Dr Hughes has had a terrible shock, Chief Inspector. He needs to be examined by a doctor. He's in no condition to be answering questions. I suggest you continue this tomorrow.'

Ms Bingham had not asked Hughes anything in order to find out what he wanted or needed. She was taking control of the situation and he seemed happy to go along with what she was saying, happy to have the responsibility of any decision taken from him.

They couldn't insist on continuing the interview. They had no evidence that Hughes was involved in the attack on his wife. The barrister was acting as if she expected him to be treated as a grieving husband, not a suspect. Gawn wondered if she knew he and Harriet had split up. She allowed herself to speculate on exactly what Ms Bingham's relationship with Hughes might be. They had certainly seemed like very good friends when she was clutching his head to her bosom.

Gawn pointed out that Hughes would need to be examined by a police doctor and his clothes taken for forensic examination. She could see that Natalie Bingham would have loved to thwart them but she was experienced enough to know which battles to fight and when to surrender gracefully. She had stopped them questioning him any further just now. That was all she could do for today. As they left the room, Natalie Bingham made it clear Hughes would present himself at Police Headquarters the next morning at eleven with his solicitor.

Once the front door was closed behind them and they were outside away from any other ears, Gawn turned to Maxwell.

'I'm surprised you didn't remember Ms Bingham, Paul. She's not exactly easy to miss, is she?'

'I was up to my eyes at the time we met. Under a lot of pressure. Remember? The Falloon case?'

She would never forget that case. She hurried on.

'OK. We can't question him any more just now but I don't think he's likely to be going anywhere. Did you get his coat?'

'Yes. I handed it over to Forensics.'

'Had Mrs Bingham done anything to it?'

'No. She didn't have the chance.'

'Good. Get someone to do a full background check on Hughes so we know what we're dealing with when we talk to him tomorrow. I know what Jenny told me about him but I'd like independent corroboration. Get them to check if he has any criminal record especially for violence and especially violence against women. Then we'll see what story his clothes tell us of what happened here.'

'What are you going to do now?' Maxwell asked.

'I'm going to Jenny's.'

'Do you think she's there?'

'I don't know but if she isn't I'll see if I can get inside and have a look around.'

'Without a search warrant?' His voice betrayed his disapproval.

'I'm quite friendly with Jenny's neighbour, Victoria, and I think she keeps a spare key for her. I won't touch anything but I can cast an eye over the place; see if there's anything to show us where she might be or if something's happened to her.'

'What do you want me to do?' he asked.

'Could you check in at the PM, Paul? I'd prefer not to have to listen to Munroe bad-mouthing Jenny but we need to get a definite time of death and cause as soon as possible. And see if Lyons' team has turned up a murder weapon yet.'

'Will do, boss.'

Chapter 8

It seemed strange to be in Jenny's apartment when she wasn't there. It felt empty and sad but Gawn thought she was probably just being over-sensitive, letting her imagination and her anxieties take over.

She liked Jenny Norris. They had struck up an easy friendship when the pathologist had moved back to Northern Ireland from Boston to cover Munroe's sabbatical and although Gawn had been back living in Northern Ireland for some time by then she had made no real friends. She hadn't really wanted to. She had always found relationships messy. But Jenny had been different right from the start. She was fun, easy-going and undemanding as a friend. She had been prepared to accept Gawn just as she was and let her keep private the darker sides of her life which she didn't share with anyone. Somehow Gawn had trusted her.

Jenny Norris was the first person she had spoken to about her feelings for Sebastian York, the first who knew they were married and she had also entrusted her with the secret that they were trying to start a family. So it was Jenny who had spent most of yesterday with her while she endured a barrage of tests at a private fertility clinic in Dublin. Gawn thought of herself as a good judge of character. She didn't like to think Jenny could kill someone and then run away.

The lounge, with its tiny kitchen area, was tidy just as Jenny kept her lab. A place for everything. Well-organised.

Only one rinsed mug sat out beside the sink, washed but not put away. A large cardboard box was sitting in the middle of the floor. Gawn looked inside. It was empty. No evidence of what it had contained.

She moved to the bedroom. When she opened the door and looked in, it told a very different story. It was obvious something had gone on here. A scene of devastation lay before her. Was it Jenny in a hurry trying to escape in a panic after killing Harriet, or had there been some sort of a struggle? And, if so, who had Jenny been struggling with?

Gawn stood back and tried to take it all in. Clothes were strewn over the bed and floor, pulled out of opened drawers and simply discarded. The wardrobe door was lying ajar. The bedclothes were lying on the floor too, revealing the bare mattress. Coiled springs were visible where the mattress cover had been sliced open. This wasn't Jenny panicking. Or someone fighting. Someone had been searching for something.

Everything had been swept off the top of the dressing table. Gawn saw a smashed photo frame lying by the side of the bed. She took out her phone and photographed its position. She was already wearing a pair of nitrile gloves. She picked it up. The picture was a selfie of Jenny and Harriet. The pathologist had her arm around Harriet's shoulder. They were both smiling broadly. They were casually dressed and Gawn knew the two women shared a passion for hill walking. This looked as if it had been taken somewhere in Mourne country. They were happy and relaxed, enjoying each other's company. Gawn realised it could be interpreted as a couple depending how you wanted to present it. She returned the frame back to the floor ensuring it was as close to its original position as possible, checking it against the photograph she had taken.

Back in the lounge, ignoring her promise to touch nothing, Gawn began looking through drawers and opening cupboards. Nothing seemed to have been disturbed. It had not been subject to a search as the bedroom had. But this was too good an opportunity to miss and she might get a clue where to find her friend. She just needed to find something to get her started.

When she thought there was nowhere else to look and she was about to leave it to the CSIs, she remembered the old chair in the guest bedroom. When she opened the door, it was obvious someone had been looking in here too. Unlike Jenny's room the sparse furnishings left few hiding places. The mattress was askew. The bedclothes had been pulled off and lay in a pile on the floor. The drawers in the bedside cabinet were pulled open and the single chair had been tipped onto its side.

The chair looked like a Lloyd Loom design but she remembered Jenny proudly explaining to her that it was a special one-off replica that she had bought in a vintage store on a weekend trip to the Hamptons. She loved it and thought it very clever. It had been specially constructed for an eccentric elderly gentleman who had an aversion to banks and wanted to keep his valuables at home without the expense of having a safe fitted. So the seat cushion could be lifted off if you found the concealed switch revealing a secret space inside. Jenny had demonstrated it to her and explained she was using it to hide her treasures. Gawn remembered advising her that evening to get a safe fitted as soon as possible but Jenny had just laughed. She had nothing worth stealing, she said. She was using it for personal papers. Nothing else. She didn't have any valuables.

Whoever had been searching had not known about the chair, had merely thrown it over out of the way or perhaps in anger. Now Gawn hesitated before working at the mechanism, her fingers seeking the elusive switch which Jenny had seemed to find so easily. She was almost about to give up when she heard a soft click and felt the cushion move under her hand. She lifted it out of its frame.

Below was an unexpectedly deep space. She picked up the contents and spread them out on the bed. There were various documents and papers, something which looked like a typical jewellery box and another box made of polished wood.

Gawn sat down on the side of the bed and began leafing through the papers. It felt so intrusive. Jenny was her friend. These things were private but it was likely that within a day or two her team would be doing this, prying into every corner of her friend's life.

The first papers she lifted were documents registering Jenny's medical qualifications and copies of her references from the Medical Examiner's Office in Boston. There was a copy of her will and also her British passport. At least she wouldn't be able to fly off somewhere although she wouldn't need a passport to get the ferry to Scotland or head south over the border. Whatever had happened last night she hadn't intended to flee abroad afterwards. The rest were personal letters and Gawn didn't want to read through these… yet. She would do it, if it became necessary.

She turned to the jewellery box and opened the lid. A dainty ballerina in a pretty pink tutu started pirouetting and a jingly tune played. She'd had one just like this when she was a little girl. The tune was Fleur de Lis, she remembered. She glanced briefly inside but there was nothing of interest or great value, it seemed. Jenny didn't go in for expensive or flashy jewellery.

She was almost about to close the lid again when her attention was caught by a simple gold necklace with an unusual knot design hanging off the chain. She had seen it before in the photograph on the bedroom floor. In fact, she now realised she had seen two of them, Jenny and Harriet had been wearing matching necklaces. She brought out her phone and googled 'necklace with knot' and her eyes widened as she recognised the image on the screen and read the message which came with it:

No matter where you go
No matter what you do
Our friendship means
That I will always be there for you.

This rhyme sounded more like the mantra Gawn and her husband shared that he would love her 'no matter what'. Had Jenny and Harriet been closer than she had been led to believe?

The final item she turned her attention to was the highly polished cherry wood box with an inlay design of a single yellow rose. It was an expensive piece, she thought, the carving delicate. Probably something else Jenny had bought on one of her antique-hunting trips in New England. It didn't seem particularly heavy and Gawn, having noticed the keyhole, expected it to be locked. Instead it opened easily to her touch. She lifted the lid to reveal an empty space. There was nothing inside but the bright red silk lining. The box might be empty now but Gawn recognised the outline of what it had once held. She was in no doubt that this box had, at least at one time, held a handgun. What was going on? Why had Jenny felt she needed a gun? Where had she got it and more urgently where was it now?

Chapter 9

It was nearly 4pm. Maxwell had gathered the team together for an update. They had already started when Gawn arrived and she slipped into the back of the room not wanting to cause a distraction. Maxwell spotted her immediately and raised his eyebrows at her in question. She gave a barely perceptible shake of her head.

'OK, Billy. What have you got on Dr Hughes then?' Maxwell asked.

Harriet Hughes' picture took central position on the murder board alongside that of her husband. There were photos from the crime scene too including some from the drone which showed the interior, or what was left of it, through the gaping opening in the roof.

Harriet had been an attractive woman. Her dark hair hung down over her shoulders and her soulful eyes looked out at the assembled detectives. Gawn remembered from their brief meeting in the John Hewitt bar how those eyes had twinkled with excitement as she talked about the potential customer for her artwork.

DC Billy Logan remained seated at his desk but he swivelled in his chair to face his colleagues, enjoying being the centre of attention. He noticed the DCI at the back of the room and sat up a little straighter.

'Edward Malcolm Hughes, born in Ballymena, 4th March 1977. Educated locally and then university in Edinburgh. He got a first-class honours degree in genetics. Whatever that is. He met his wife, Harriet, our victim, when she was studying at the College of Art there. They married in 2005 in Scotland. Moved back here then and set up home in Bangor. He's worked for a number of different companies until he joined Altor Pharmaceuticals in 2015. He's been there ever since. Mrs Hughes began teaching in Manor Hill Special School as soon as she came here and stayed there until just a couple of weeks ago. They have no children. They still live in the same house in Bangor but from what one of the neighbours told us Mrs Hughes hasn't been around the place for over a month. No one has seen her. The neighbours say they were a nice ordinary couple. And that's about all we've got so far.'

Logan's voice trailed off but then he added, 'We haven't approached any of his work colleagues yet. We weren't sure how you wanted to play it. Whether we should speak to them or not.'

'No, we don't want to be too heavy-handed or give his solicitor any reason to complain. He's a person of interest but we've nothing definite yet to tie him to the attack, have we? Or the arson? No forensics?' Maxwell queried.

No one responded to his questions.

'Does Hughes have any kind of criminal record, Billy?' Gawn asked. Heads turned when she spoke. Most of the others hadn't realised she was there, listening.

'No, ma'am. The inspector asked me to check. There's nothing in our records here. I could check with Police Scotland.'

'Do. If there is anything, it's probably just the usual student stuff. Drunkenness or behaviour likely to cause a breach of the peace at some student protest or other. But best to check. What about our victim? Have we made any progress on her background yet?'

Detective Sergeant Erin McKeown took over. 'We've managed to trace Harriet Hughes or Harriet Wright as she was then in London, ma'am. She was living there with her parents when she was about five. Their names were Charles and Eleanor Wright. Father was an executive in the oil industry. Mrs Wright was British but Mr Wright was American and it's possible Harriet was born in the States. We haven't found a birth certificate for her in the UK yet. She went to the local primary school in Chigwell and then to a girls' boarding school in Cheltenham. The family seemed to be pretty well-off. She even spent a year at a private college in Switzerland after she left school before going to art college in Edinburgh. The Wrights had no other children and they're both dead now.'

'I suppose you'd better try to check with the American authorities about where she was born, but it's not a priority. Don't waste too much time on it, Erin. Where she was born won't have anything to do with her death now,' Maxwell said. 'And we'd better look into her finances in case someone, other than her husband, benefits from her death.'

Still standing at the back of the room, Gawn asked, 'What about this Altor Pharmaceuticals, Billy? I haven't heard of them.'

'They're involved in "cutting edge research" according to their website.' The veteran detective moved his fingers to mimic a set of quotation marks. 'Gene therapy.' He shrugged, displaying his usual cynicism.

'Hardly anything that would have got Mrs Hughes killed,' Maxwell said.

'I agree. Have we heard anything at all from Forensics yet?'

Gawn moved across the room as she spoke and stood beside Maxwell in front of the display of photographs. Although it had only been a few hours since the discovery of the body, her impatience was already growing. The beginning of any new case was always a frustrating time until they had something definite, a strong line of inquiry. This time she was especially anxious because of Jenny's involvement and from the way things were looking she seemed to be a likely suspect.

'No, ma'am. Not about the murder but they've suggested that one of the sets of tyre tracks came from a four-wheel-drive vehicle.' McKeown paused and then added, 'Probably a Land Rover.'

Gawn's mind went immediately to an image of Jenny Norris' battered old Land Rover. It had often been a source for comment but the pathologist liked its solid strength and argued that it meant she could deal with any terrain on a call-out, no matter how challenging. Gawn could see significant looks passing between the others in the room. Word had got around already that Jenny Norris was involved in some way. She should have expected it. They were good detectives after all, handpicked. They all knew the pathologist drove a Land Rover. They had seen her coming and going from crime scenes often enough in the battered green vehicle which she had nicknamed Betsey. But then hundreds of other people, especially in the countryside, drove Land Rovers. It didn't mean it was Jenny who had been at the scene around the time of the murder but she knew Jenny had been there sometime on Monday evening and left her phone behind, so it probably was her car that had made the tracks. It just didn't prove she had come back again to kill Harriet. But it was something they couldn't overlook, Gawn realised.

'Should we put out a call for Dr Norris' Land Rover, boss?'

Maxwell was asking the question in front of all the others. He hadn't explained why he was making the sudden jump from a report of a four-wheel drive vehicle to this question about Jenny Norris' Land Rover. No one questioned him and Gawn knew exactly what he was doing. He was forcing her hand. She couldn't be seen to be showing any favouritism. She needed to follow procedure. After all Jenny could be a victim or at the very least a witness to the events at the bungalow.

Everyone seemed to be waiting for what she would say next. She could almost feel them holding their breath although she knew that was nonsense. They weren't. They couldn't know all the details of how involved the pathologist might be. No one did. Not Maxwell. And not even herself yet, she thought.

'Do it.'

Maxwell swung into action. 'Right. We need feet on the ground. Go back and see who you can get to speak to tonight. Then mop up anyone you can't get first thing in the morning. We know our vic was alive around 9.30 last night.' Maxwell glanced across at Gawn as he said this but didn't explain how he knew to the others. 'The husband arrived around seven this morning according to when he put the emergency call through to the Fire Service. So we have a window of around nine or ten hours. Hopefully the PM will be able to cut that down even further. In the meantime, someone needs to question all the neighbours, fully this time. There are the Binghams who seem to have known both Hughes and his wife in some way and who came over when they saw the smoke. I spoke to Mr Bingham this morning but only very briefly. Has anyone taken a statement from them yet?'

He looked around but got no response.

'They need to be interviewed. We need to know if they saw anything out of the ordinary before they noticed the fire; if they'd seen anyone hanging about recently for example, maybe watching the house. There are another couple of houses at the bottom of the lane too. Those people need to be questioned as well. Did they see or hear anything late on Monday night or early on Tuesday morning? There can't be much traffic passing on that road, so they might have noticed something. There's a garage on the main road not too far away from the lane. It would be too much to hope our perp stopped there for petrol but there could be some CCTV which might cover part of the road as well and could maybe pick up a bit of the passing traffic. Someone needs to check that and, if there is any, have a look at it. Erin, can I leave it to you to sort out who does what?'

'On it, sir.'

Chapter 10

While Maxwell had been issuing his orders, Gawn had slipped out again and made her way to her own office. She was not surprised when the door opened a few minutes later and Maxwell walked in.

'I take it Jenny wasn't in her apartment?' he asked immediately.

'No.' Her response was flat. Her voice might be expressionless but her face revealed how worried she was. She was seated behind her desk almost using it as a barrier between herself and Maxwell.

'Did you manage to get in and have a look around?' he asked.

'Yes. Jenny's neighbour was most helpful. I spun her a story about leaving a ring there when I'd stayed over and she let me in. Remind me to tell Jenny to warn Victoria not to be so trusting in future.'

As she said it, she hoped she would have the opportunity to have that conversation with her friend over a glass of wine in her apartment when all this was over, and whoever had bludgeoned Harriet Hughes to death was caught.

'And?' He waited for her to continue. When she didn't respond immediately, he added, 'What did you find, Gawn?'

She had promised not to touch anything but he knew it would be too much of a temptation to be there and do nothing. She would have searched, taking care not to disturb anything, of course. Now she was hiding something from him. She had found something. He knew, so he just waited. She would tell him. He thought she might try to hide things from him sometimes, but she wouldn't lie directly to him. At least he didn't think so. She had obviously found something which she wasn't rushing to share.

'At first, I thought it looked like she'd left in a hurry or maybe there'd been a struggle. The apartment looked as if it might have been searched but there were no signs of a break-in. I checked the lock on the front door. But her bedroom was in quite a state. A mess. Stuff all over the floor including a smashed picture and I don't think Jenny would have done it.'

If she was mentioning the picture, it meant it had some significance.

'A picture of what?' Maxwell asked.

'Of the two of them. Jenny and Harriet together.'

'Knocked over in some kind of struggle?'

'Or smashed in anger,' she reluctantly conceded.

He raised his eyebrows at her but said nothing.

'And I found a wooden box,' she said.

'Yes?'

It felt like he was having to drag everything out of her. She realised he would want to know what was in the box. He would realise it must be something important or she wouldn't be so reticent about telling him, offering the information about a smashed picture first which was circumstantial as regards motive but potentially damning enough.

'It was empty… but I'm pretty sure it had contained a gun. I just couldn't tell how recently.'

'Jesus! What was she doing with a gun? Does she have a licence?'

'I don't know. She never mentioned having a gun to me but it's not the sort of thing that comes up in casual conversation over a plate of spaghetti, is it?'

She realised how sarcastic she sounded. She was taking her worries out on him. Gawn was beginning to wonder what else about her friend she didn't know; what other secrets she had kept from her. She had plenty of secrets herself but somehow she had thought Jenny was an open book.

'Right' – Gawn gave herself a shake – 'get someone to check for a gun licence.' She seemed to change her mind. 'No, check yourself, Paul. Don't involve any of the others. The fewer people who know anything about a gun, the better. At least for now. Harriet wasn't shot so it probably has nothing to do with anything. Then get a search warrant and send a forensics team over to Jenny's apartment. They need, well, I don't need to tell them their job. Maybe, if we're lucky, Mark will have finished in court today and be able to go himself.'

She stood up while she was still speaking as if she needed to be moving, needed to be doing something.

'You're already having all Harriet's neighbours questioned and any traffic cameras checked. That's good. See if we can get a definite time for Hughes' arrival this morning and for any other vehicles of interest in the area. I'll probably show up on it. Warn whoever's doing the search so they don't freak out if they spot me.

'And we need to talk to the Hughes' neighbours in Bangor again to see what more they can tell us about the state of the marriage, and to Harriet's colleagues at the school in case she talked to any of them about being worried about anything or feeling threatened. We'll hold back on questioning Hughes' colleagues at Altor for a while. We don't want Ms Bingham accusing us of harassing a grieving husband.

'And we need to get hold of the CCTV from Jenny's apartment building to see the comings and goings yesterday. That should be more than enough to keep everyone busy. We have Hughes at eleven in the morning for an interview and I want to be as prepared as we can be before we speak to him again. He's still our principal suspect.'

Her words had been coming out in a rush as she thought of all that had to be done. It was just as well she hadn't been looking at Maxwell as she had been speaking because his face told a different story. Jenny Norris had to be at least an equal suspect with Harriet's husband but he didn't say anything to her. The DCI was too good a police officer not to know that. She would follow the evidence and if it led to Jenny Norris, she would do what she had to do. He had no doubt about that. She just didn't want to think about that yet. Neither did he.

* * *

'Have they sent over the recording of the 999 call yet?'

'Yes. It came through about half an hour ago.'

'Have you listened to it, Paul?'

'Not yet.'

'Let's do it now.'

They moved to Maxwell's office and he sat down at his computer and clicked the recording icon. A woman's calm voice spoke first.

> *'Which service do you require?'*

> *'Fire. I need the Fire Service. The house is on fire.'*

Edward Hughes' voice sounded breathy and agitated.

'Does he sound distressed to you, Paul?'

'Hard to tell. A bit. Maybe. I don't know him well enough to make a judgement.'

> *'Fire Service. What's your name?'*

> *'My name? What does my friggin' name matter?'*

> *'We just need the details, sir.'*

> *'Hughes. Edward Hughes.'*

> *'What is the address of the property, Mr Hughes?'*

Gawn half-expected Hughes to correct the woman and demand to be called doctor. But he didn't.

> *'Mourneview Loanen, Drumarity.'*

> *'What's the house number, sir?'*

> *'Number? Number? I don't know a number. There's only a couple of houses on the friggin' lane for God's sake. They can't miss it. Get them here before the whole place goes up.'*

> *'Can you give me a postcode?'*

> *'I don't know the friggin' postcode.'*

> *'Are you out of the building, sir, or still inside?'*

'What? Yes. Yes, of course, I'm out. I wasn't in the building. I've only just arrived.'

Paul paused the playback to make a comment.

'That supports what he told us. Why bother telling the operator that?'

'Why indeed, unless you wanted to establish you'd just arrived?'

'You really think he's as devious and premeditated as that?' he asked.

'If he'd killed his wife the previous evening, he'd have had all night to work out what he should say. Everyone knows 999 calls are recorded. Maybe he worked out how to act like a distraught husband.'

Even to her own ears that sounded a bit far-fetched.

'That's cold. You really fancy him for this, don't you, boss?'

'Don't you, Paul? You know the statistics on murders; how many victims know their killers, especially spouses and partners.'

They both knew the figures. A high percentage of murder victims knew their attacker but they weren't all spouses. It was true for partners, boyfriends and girlfriends, siblings even, parents too. So that didn't preclude Jenny, if she had been in a relationship with the dead woman, but Maxwell didn't mention that to her. He didn't think she'd want to hear it and he knew the truth was Gawn wasn't sure if it was Hughes who had killed Harriet. She just didn't want it to be Jenny Norris. Neither did he, of course.

Maxwell started the recording again.

'Is there anyone still inside the building, Mr Hughes?'

'Look, are you sending help? Hurry up for God's sake.'

Hughes was shouting now.

'The fire brigade is on its way, sir, is anyone still inside the premises?'

'What?'

'Is there anyone still inside the premises?'

'My wife. God, my wife, Harriet, she's in there. Please get them here quickly.'

'They're on their way sir. Just stay on the line.'

'It sounds genuine enough,' Maxwell suggested as he clicked to stop the playback.

'What time was the call logged?' Gawn asked.

'7.04.'

'OK. It backs up what he said about the time he arrived. If he phoned as soon as he got there.'

'And it does sound like he thought his wife was inside and that he didn't know she was lying up the lane.'

'Maybe. But he wasn't even thinking of Harriet at first. He was focused on getting them to come and put the fire out. It was only when the operator asked if anyone was still inside the building that he remembered his wife. Remember what I said at the scene? Just think how you would sound if Kerri was in a burning building and you were outside. I know how I would sound if Seb was.'

'Except you wouldn't be outside just waiting, would you, boss?'

Chapter 11

Early Wednesday morning Gawn was at her desk reading reports that had come in overnight. The squad room was empty. McKeown had arranged for anyone not contacted yesterday to be interviewed this morning.

Just after eight o'clock Maxwell knocked the door and walked in carrying two cups. Steam was rising from them. He handed one across to her.

'I see you've already had one.' He nodded at an empty mug sitting on her desk.

'Just about ready for another.' She smiled at him and took the cup from his hand. 'Thank you.'

She looked tired. He had mentioned to Kerri that he was worried about her. Her curt reply had been that Gawn was not his responsibility to worry about. She had a husband. Kerri said Gawn was probably worried Seb was having too good a time in Hollywood with all the wannabe actresses throwing themselves at him to be bothered about missing her. But Paul didn't think Seb would be likely to cheat on her. He hoped not. He didn't think she would cope very well if he did.

'One piece of good news,' he announced with a smile.

'Yes?'

'Jenny does have a licence for a personal protection weapon. No indication of why she needed it but apparently she'd brought it with her from Boston and had permission to bring it into the country so maybe she'd needed it there. Anyhow she keeps it at a local gun club now so that's one thing less for us to worry about. Anything in that lot?'

He indicated the sheaf of papers in front of her on the desk.

'Not much. Jo and Walter went back and interviewed Mr and Mrs Bingham last night. It seems they've known Edward Hughes and his parents for years and that's how they'd met Harriet. When Harriet was looking for somewhere to live, Mr Bingham offered her the bungalow next to theirs. They own both of them. Jo says here she got the impression Mrs Bingham didn't seem too enamoured of Harriet and Edward being together. She seems to be Hughes' number one fan. She also let slip that at one time they had hoped that Hughes and their daughter Natalie might have got together, which links in with the vibes I was getting from Natalie Bingham yesterday when we were talking to her.'

'Any sightings of Jenny's Land Rover?' Maxwell asked, changing the subject.

He assumed she wouldn't be keen to tell him about it if it reflected badly on the pathologist. She might want to put off telling him but he needed to know. He wasn't going to let her throw away her career trying to defend her friend.

'Not yet. But Erin got hold of the CCTV footage from her apartment building.'

'And?' he prompted.

'Jenny went out first thing on Monday morning, shortly after seven. Erin doesn't know where she went.'

Gawn did.

'She was back before six in the evening carrying some bags,' she continued. 'Erin hasn't tried to find where she spent the day yet but it's probably not relevant. It looked like she'd been shopping.'

Maxwell thought she sounded evasive and she hadn't met his eye as she'd been speaking.

'I suppose we might need to do that but I don't think it's a high priority.' Gawn paused. 'Anyway she left again just after 9.30 that evening. She was caught on camera driving out of the car park. She looked upset and in a hurry, according to Erin. After that, nothing. I'll have to have a look at the footage myself.'

She didn't seem to be looking forward to that.

'Where is she, Gawn? Where would she go? You know her better than anyone else.'

He dropped down into the armchair across the desk from her and took a sip of his tea. It was hot and he blew on it to cool it down.

'I thought I did but maybe I don't. She talked about friends but they were all just casual acquaintances. She was good at making friends wherever she went. She talked about her family but she's been estranged from them ever since she came out. I can't see her turning to them if she was in trouble but I suppose they do say blood is thicker than water so, maybe in a crisis, she would.'

'Someone should speak to them then.' Maxwell looked at her pointedly.

'By someone, I take it, you mean me?'

He didn't reply. He didn't need to.

'Meanwhile what are you going to be doing?' she asked.

'I'm heading back over to the mortuary. I didn't wait for Munroe to finish the PM yesterday. You know he doesn't like to have someone standing looking over his shoulder, harassing him as he calls it, but he promised to have the report ready first thing this morning. Strangely enough, he seemed to want to do whatever he could to help Jenny. He said he'd put a rush on everything and get it finished for us. So, I'm going to go across and make sure he does.'

'OK. Meet back here at 10.30 before we tackle the grieving husband.'

Chapter 12

Gawn had been rehearsing in her mind what she would say to Jenny Norris' parents while she drove over the Craigantlet Hills taking the back route to Bangor avoiding the busy A2. No enjoying the views of the rolling fields of the County Down countryside this morning. She barely even noticed them and focused only on driving.

By the time she had negotiated the Bangor ring road and was approaching the development of detached houses and bungalows where Jenny's parents lived, on the far side of the town heading towards Donaghadee, she had made up her mind to be as direct as possible. There was no point in pussyfooting around.

The Norris' home was a two-storey detached house in a mock Tudor development, one of the many new estates in the area. Building work was still going on further along the road and a bulldozer was sitting parked in front of their house. The road was covered in muddy tracks left by the construction traffic and the noise of drilling and hammering echoed up the street. Gawn walked up the paved pathway wondering what these people would be like. She noted that although they were living in what was essentially a building site, they had wasted no time settling in and their garden was already neatly turfed and beds dug out. Low shrubs formed a barrier to mark out their plot.

Jenny had spoken of her parents but not often. It was an obvious source of sadness to her to have been disowned by her family. Gawn pressed the doorbell, noticing it was one with a camera. No doubt somewhere within the building someone was watching her and wondering who she was and what she wanted.

It was early and Gawn wondered if the couple might still be in bed. Within a minute, however, the door opened and a woman's slightly anxious face appeared around the side of the frame. Up to today, Gawn had given Jenny's parents no thought. She had never considered what they would look like so she was surprised to see a face so like Jenny's that it would be impossible to hide their relationship. It was like looking at Jenny thirty years in the future, Jenny with some grey hairs showing through the blond and some wrinkles giving even more character to her friendly face.

'Yes? Can I help you?' The voice was quiet, refined, friendly but displaying a certain wariness.

'Mrs Norris?'

The woman nodded.

'Yes.'

'I'm DCI Gawn Girvin.'

A man's brusque voice sounded from inside the building. 'Who is it, Felicity?'

'It's the police, dear.'

Almost immediately a male materialised in the doorway. He was broader and taller than his wife for Gawn had no doubt this was Mr Norris. Jenny had described her father as severe and daunting. He had been the headmaster of a boys' school, a figure of authority and he had carried that same authority home with him, organising his home and his two daughters in the same way.

'Do you have any identification?' he asked.

Hastily she pulled her ID from her pocket and held it out to him.

He perused it carefully.

'Thank you. You can't be too careful these days. All kinds of scammers and tricksters about. Now, what can we do for you, officer? Is this about setting up Neighbourhood Watch?'

'May I come in, sir? I need to speak to you about your daughter.'

'Melanie? Has something happened to Melanie?' The woman's voice had risen an octave as she reached round to take her husband's arm for support.

Gawn knew Melanie was Jenny's sister. Jenny had told her the sisters had met up secretly a few times since she had moved back to Northern Ireland.

'No. It's not Melanie. It's Jenny.'

Gawn could see the relief on their faces. According to Jenny, Melanie had always been the favourite child at least for their father – the one who followed the path set out for her, the one who had matched the expectations of staying in Northern Ireland, living nearby, marrying a stolid local man with good prospects, providing two adorable grandchildren, taking the usual, in Jenny's words, boring route, not rushing off to the other side of the world to cut up dead people and definitely not bringing shame on the family's name by coming out to the world as gay.

It was an old-fashioned viewpoint in the twenty-first century but Gawn knew there were still plenty of people in Northern Ireland who subscribed to it. She knew homophobic crimes were on the rise and even more were going unreported. Perhaps then it wasn't really surprising that a parent wouldn't want their child to have to face all the difficulties and dangers associated with being honest about their sexuality.

'Our daughter Jennifer is in America. We don't know anything about her.'

'Actually she's not. Dr Norris has been back in Northern Ireland for nearly a year now.'

Gawn could see the shock on their faces at her words. They obviously weren't poker players and they knew nothing about Jenny and what was going on in her life. Wherever she had gone for help, it wasn't to these people, Gawn was sure.

They were still all standing on the doorstep and it seemed she was not going to be invited inside. She pulled a business card from her pocket.

'We need to speak with Dr Norris urgently. If she does happen to get in touch, could you ask her to contact me, please? It's very important.'

She held out the business card and Mrs Norris took it from her.

'Thank you,' Gawn said and turned and walked back to her car. She was sure they were watching but she didn't turn around to look. Meeting Jenny's parents had helped her understand her friend a little better. So, if she wouldn't go to them for help, where would she go?

She thought of Jenny's sister, Melanie, and wondered if she should contact her. With a husband who was a member of the local Legislative Assembly with a high public profile and two small children who wouldn't be good at keeping secrets, she decided it was unlikely Jenny was hiding out at her house. She might need to question her later but not now. Now she needed to get back to meet

Hughes and his solicitor. She was looking forward to the meeting. She had lots of questions for him.

Chapter 13

It was a few minutes after 10.30 when Gawn arrived back. She was just about to lift the phone and let Maxwell know when she heard a knock and the door opened.

'Spotted you arriving in the car park,' he announced by way of explanation for his timely appearance.

'I hope you got something useful from Munroe because I drew a blank with Jenny's parents. They haven't seen her. She hasn't been in touch and they didn't seem much interested in finding out anything about her. They didn't even know she was back in the country, for God's sake, and they never asked why we were looking for her.' She sounded annoyed.

'Well, I've got us a time of death. Munroe puts it at between 8pm and midnight as he thought yesterday and, when I pushed him, he said he'd favour the earlier end of the time range.'

'That's impossible. She couldn't have been killed at eight o'clock or even nine. We know she was alive around 9.30. She must have been attacked very soon after I was there to fit in with Munroe's timings. We'll see where Hughes says he was between eight and midnight. Probably at home in bed, I would guess. But maybe we'll turn up someone who saw comings and goings at the bungalow around then. If we're lucky. What about the cause of death?'

'It was blunt force trauma to the head. The back of her head was smashed in – more than one blow – but there was also an injury to her temple and Lyons's team found blood on the edge of a table in the living room. They've sent it for matching. There seemed to be some signs of a struggle although it was a bit difficult to tell with the firemen being all through the place, but it looks like that's where she was injured first. Munroe says from that initial injury he estimates she would have been able to run away. She wouldn't necessarily have been knocked unconscious. Probably not. It was just a glancing blow.' Maxwell finished and waited for a response.

'So, she fights with someone. She was either pushed or she fell and hit her head on the table. It could have been an accident. Then she runs trying to get away from whoever she'd fought with. They chase her, catch up with her and hit her from behind, which definitely couldn't have been an accident. With what? Do we know, Paul? Have they found a weapon yet?'

'Not yet but Munroe says from traces he found in the wound he'd be confident it was a rock of some kind.'

'So, something that was to hand. Not a weapon brought especially, and probably just flung away somewhere afterwards.'

'Yes. They're still working at the crime scene but it could have been flung out of a car window miles away and they wouldn't be able to get fingerprints from a piece of rock anyway.'

'Maybe not but they might get blood or DNA or something. If there was a struggle the attacker might have been hurt too. There could be injuries on our perp as well.'

'Can we examine Hughes' hands when we talk to him?' Maxwell asked.

'We don't need to. The doctor will have done it yesterday. Get hold of his report and check if he noted any injuries, and put a rocket under the lab to get results of any swabs taken. Have Hughes and his solicitor arrived yet?'

'Yes. Just before I came in here,' Maxwell said.

'Do we know who his solicitor is?'

'Why do you ask?'

'Because if "my learned friend" Ms Bingham has had anything to do with it I would expect he's some big criminal lawyer with plenty of experience and he'll not be letting us get away with anything.'

Chapter 14

Gawn was right.

They had stopped in Comms and were watching Hughes and his solicitor in the interview room. They both recognised the older man. He was Jerome Hartnett. Never Jerry. Always Jerome. One half of Hartnett & Magill, a heavyweight law firm which dealt exclusively with criminal cases and had offices in Belfast and Dublin. He was a rather pompous and flamboyant figure, well known around the High Court for his expensive suits with a silk hankie always in the top pocket and a matching colourful silk tie.

But he was also well known as an extremely successful solicitor. He had been associated with some of the most high-profile cases and some of the most notorious figures in Northern Ireland crime circles over the last fifteen years, including Edmund Falloon who was still on remand in Dublin awaiting extradition to Belfast for the murder of a student twenty years ago. It had been the case which had nearly broken Gawn; the one she still had flashbacks about.

Everyone suspected Hartnett had links to organised crime but he was too clever to ever get his own hands dirty. Not a man to be underestimated.

Hartnett was sitting casually twiddling his gold pen between his fingers, looking supremely relaxed. The interview room was his domain. He felt comfortable here, at home, looking forward to the battle of minds to come. Hughes, on the other hand, looked ill. He was obviously nervous and twice already, while they had been watching, they had seen Hartnett reach across and pat his client's arm in an encouraging gesture trying to calm his anxieties.

'How do you want to play this, boss?'

'Very carefully, Paul. Hartnett's a wily old goat. We overstep an inch and old Jerry will have Hughes out of here in a flash. He's the grieving husband, right? He should be really keen to help us catch his wife's killer. That's the line. Let's see what he has to say for himself.'

And she took a deep breath.

* * *

The two men's heads came up in unison like a pair of synchronised swimmers. Hughes looked even more tense and uncomfortable when he saw who it was. He was out of his element. Hartnett, on the other hand, exuded confidence. He even managed a smile of sorts – well, what passed for a smile with him, his mouth slightly open and a row of perfectly straight white teeth displayed, rather like a shark circling for the kill.

'Good morning, Dr Hughes.' Gawn was careful to give him his title. 'Good morning, Mr Hartnett.'

'Good morning, Chief Inspector, Inspector.' Hartnett's eyes passed from Gawn to Maxwell, greeting them both. Those eyes were cold, a steely grey as they surveyed the two police officers.

Hughes didn't speak.

'Thank you for coming in,' Gawn said. 'We appreciate your help, sir.'

'Have you caught Mrs Hughes' killer yet, Chief Inspector?' the solicitor asked, a thin smile forming on his lips.

Was Hartnett taunting them? He knew that a spouse was always the most likely suspect and would have to be eliminated from their inquiries.

'No, sir. We're following various lines of inquiry but it would be really useful to hear what your client can add to our understanding of what happened on Monday night.' Gawn kept her voice neutral.

'My client found his wife's body yesterday morning, not Monday night.'

'Indeed, sir, we know that but we believe Dr Hughes was at his wife's home on Monday night too and perhaps it would be best to let him speak for himself. I'm sure he would be happy to do that. He has nothing to hide and he must want his wife's killer found.'

She swivelled in her chair away from the solicitor's gaze to face Hughes directly and locked eyes with him. She smiled in what she hoped was an encouraging way. Hartnett obviously wanted to control the interview. Would he let Hughes speak?

'Of course I want to find her killer. I have nothing to hide,' Hughes almost shouted at them before Hartnett could intervene by putting his hand on his client's arm.

Gawn doubted what he had said. Everyone had something to hide about something, even her, and especially about this case.

'You were there on Monday evening, sir?' she asked.

There was a pause. Would he deny it? She knew that Hughes had been back at the house harassing Harriet that evening. Jenny had said so when she phoned and asked Gawn to go and speak to her. But they had no corroborating evidence yet. He might just deny it.

'Yes, I was. But only for a short time. Just a couple of minutes. I needed to discuss something with my wife.'

'But you were living apart, sir?'

'Yes.'

If he wondered how she knew, he didn't ask.

'We were going through a rough patch. Every marriage does, doesn't it? Women take odd notions at certain times in their lives.'

He looked at Maxwell as he spoke, seemingly in the hope of eliciting some male solidarity with his suggestion.

'It wouldn't have lasted, you know. I think Harriet was having some sort of mid-life crisis or she was going through the menopause or something. She'd thrown up her job, a job she'd always loved, and moved out of our comfortable home to live there in the back of beyond and paint. My God, who makes a living painting? I mean she could draw OK but she was no Michelangelo or Tracy Emin.' He gave a mirthless laugh.

'Did you argue about that?' Gawn asked.

'My client did not have an argument with his wife on Monday night, Chief Inspector. They were on good terms. He merely needed to have her sign some papers for his business. That's all their meeting was about.'

'Was Mrs Hughes involved in your business, sir?' Gawn continued her questioning, ignoring the solicitor and wanting to follow this new line of inquiry. They had had no idea that Harriet Hughes was involved in her husband's business. In fact they didn't even know Hughes had a business of his own. Billy had reported only that he worked for Altor Pharmaceuticals.

'I'm setting up my own company. I'm fed up with everybody else profiting from my hard work. I needed Harriet's signature on some documents. That's all. It was all perfectly amicable. We were going to get back together. I told you. It was just a matter of time until she came to her senses.'

'So when you left her on Monday night… what time would that have been, sir?' asked Maxwell.

'Around nine o'clock or 9.30, more or less. I was home and in bed just after eleven.'

Gawn realised she must have just missed him. She had been there shortly after 9.30. That was probably why Harriet hadn't let her in. She may have been too upset after the meeting with her husband and perhaps having a row with him over these papers. But she was definitely still alive then. Gawn had seen her standing at the lighted window. She had even waved at her but Harriet had not waved back. So, she was Hughes' corroboration that his wife was alive when he left her. But he could have doubled back, she argued to herself.

'And what sort of mood was your wife in when you left her?' Maxwell asked.

'Mood?'

'Was she happy? Or maybe frightened about living in the countryside with not too many people around?'

Don't put any ideas in his head, Paul, Gawn was thinking to herself. Next thing, he'll be claiming she'd noticed strangers lurking around and Hartnett will want them searching for local villains – which they were doing anyway. John Dee was already checking up on any locals with breaking and entering convictions and any peeping Toms or anyone on the Sex Offenders Register within a ten-mile radius. Trouble was, Northern Ireland was such a small place an outsider could have come from fifty miles away or even across the border to burgle the house.

'She was just… normal. There was nothing out of the ordinary.'

'And where did you go after you left your wife?' Gawn pressed him.

'Straight home, I told you.'

'And stayed there all night?'

'Of course. I went to bed.'

'Can anyone corroborate that, Mr Hughes?'

'I find that insulting, Chief Inspector. You are insinuating that my client was being unfaithful to his wife,' Hartnett interrupted.

'I'm insinuating nothing, Mr Hartnett. I'm merely trying to establish your client's whereabouts at the time when his wife was being murdered. I don't know if he has a house guest or other family member staying with him at the minute who could corroborate his story.' She was playing the innocent.

'It is not a story and I think my client has been most cooperative. He's had a bad shock and he's still grieving. That's all the questions he'll be answering.' Hartnett began to rise from his chair and Hughes was about to follow suit.

'Just one other thing, Dr Hughes,' Gawn spoke, her authoritative voice stopping them. 'You said you hurt your shoulder trying to break the front door in.'

'Yes,' Hughes said.

'Could we have a look at the injury, sir?'

Gawn wondered if he would agree. There were no obvious marks or scratches on his hands but she hadn't read the doctor's report herself. Maybe he had noted something.

'Is this really necessary, Chief Inspector?' the solicitor queried, furrowing his brow in annoyance. 'I don't see what my client's shoulder has to do with anything. He sustained the injury after his wife was already dead.'

Hartnett was much too experienced and wily a solicitor not to know why they were asking.

Hughes stood up abruptly and tugged his jacket off in a fit of temper before Hartnett could stop him. He partially unbuttoned his shirt and slipped it off his left shoulder rather like an ingenue in a matinée film of the 1930s. They could see a small purplish bruise over the top of his shoulder near his collarbone. So, that part of his story seemed to be true.

'Looks nasty, sir. It must be sore.' She spoke sympathetically.

Just as he was pulling his shirt back on, Gawn caught a glimpse of what could be a scratch on his upper arm, perhaps made by nails? She knew if she asked him to take his shirt off, his lawyer would bluster and refuse their request.

She wondered when and how Hughes had sustained the scratch and hoped the duty doctor's report was thorough and would help them. She would double-check it. If he had noted a scrape on Tuesday morning when he had examined Hughes and taken a swab, they might have a DNA profile. It could either suggest Hughes had struggled with his wife, or that the grieving husband did have another woman in his life and he might want to get rid of Harriet quickly which could provide a motive for them. Although, as she had already left him, it seemed there wouldn't be a barrier to his having a woman friend. He wouldn't need to kill Harriet to get his freedom.

If the scrape wasn't there when the doctor had examined him, it could mean he had spent Tuesday night with another woman. Natalie Bingham? In the meantime, they needed something more to link Hughes with the events inside the house and the blood on the edge of the table, but that would be difficult. He had already admitted to being there so his fingerprints would be all over the place. They needed something more.

Chapter 15

Gawn and Maxwell were still sitting in the interview room. The two men had just left, Hartnett looking pleased with himself, Hughes just relieved to get away.

Maxwell was glancing through his case notes.

'The doctor's report noted the injury to Hughes' shoulder and a slight scrape on his upper arm. He took a swab of it in case we could get DNA.'

'Interesting but until we get a match I don't know how much further it gets us. We need to check if Munroe found anything under the victim's nails,' Gawn responded.

'He didn't. Nothing to help us anyway. We didn't really learn very much more from Hughes than we already knew.'

'I'm not so sure about that, Paul. You know the old saying – if it's not sex then it's money, and if Hughes didn't attack his wife in a jealous rage then we now know they had business dealings too. That's new. It could be something to do with money. These papers he wanted her to sign might have been a point of disagreement between them. They could have argued over them. Maybe she didn't want to sign them, whatever they were. I think it would be worthwhile to dig a little more deeply into Hughes' new business and his and his wife's finances.'

'Right. I'll put Walter on it.'

'Get him to check into Hughes' current work at Altor and whatever it is he's setting up. Setting up a company can't be cheap and divorces can be very expensive. And have someone look into his love life. Does he have another woman on the go? That would be useful to know.'

Just then the door was flung open and banged back against the wall. A breathless Jamie Grant rushed in, his face flushed.

'I hope you have a really good reason for this interruption, Detective Constable.' Gawn fixed him with a steely stare.

'They think they've found Dr Norris' Land Rover,' he almost shouted, unable to disguise his excitement.

'Where?' the pair asked in unison.

'Someone spotted it in Strangford Lough.'

'*In* the Lough?' Maxwell said.

'Yes, sir.'

'Send the coordinates to my phone. I'm driving.' He had turned to Gawn as he spoke. He'd seen her reaction to Grant's news. He thought it would be safer for him to drive.

She gave him no argument, just headed out the door.

Chapter 16

It was an even more silent journey than usual. Neither Maxwell nor Gawn was in the mood for casual chatter as they approached Newtownards, a dormitory town for commuters to Belfast rather than its previous role as the site of a market for the surrounding farms. They quickly left it behind driving out past the local bowling club and the little airfield, and began to skirt around the edge of Strangford Lough following the road towards Portaferry.

Soon they spotted flashing lights over the stretch of open water. An ambulance, two marked police cars and a recovery vehicle seemed to fill every inch of the little car park at the local sailing club. Scrabo Tower in the distance peeked out of its covering of threatening grey clouds to oversee what was happening like a nosey neighbour watching from behind net curtains.

Maxwell pulled his car tightly into the side of the road, two wheels almost in the sheugh. A constable was directing traffic keeping it moving. But they were all aware of the passengers staring out from inside the passing cars and the occasional mobile phone held up to film. Gawn flashed her ID to the constable and strode into the car park.

'Who's in charge here?' She directed her question to a group of men – a trio in diving gear and an older man. They were standing in a huddle near one of the police cars, drinking tea and laughing, trying to escape the chill wind.

The morose-looking man in a rather too tight overcoat which he had buttoned over his stomach to try to offer some protection from the chilly conditions threw the remnants of his drink onto the ground and set his cup down on the car's bonnet before moving out of the circle of men and walking towards them. He didn't rush. He looked cold and bored and as if he thought he shouldn't even be there. Gawn registered a hint of indifference, maybe even incivility in his manner as he approached her.

'I am.'

He obviously didn't recognise her or Maxwell. She thought he was treating them like concerned busybodies or maybe journalists and would just want to get rid of them.

'I am, *ma'am*.'

Almost at the exact moment she had spoken, the man's expression changed as she saw his eyes go to her PSNI pass hanging from a lanyard around her neck half hidden under her jacket.

'Sorry. I am, ma'am.' He took his hands out of his pockets.

'And you are?' She deliberately held his stare, her eyes boring into him.

He moved his hand to his collar as if it was tightening around his neck.

'McBride. John McBride, ma'am. Detective Sergeant.'

'Well, Detective Sergeant John McBride, what's happening here, apart from you all having a nice cosy tea break while I'm waiting for information on a murder case?'

She folded her arms across her chest emphasising her displeasure and impatience and stared at him as she waited for his reply.

'We got a call that there was a vehicle in the water, ma'am. The first patrol car to get here could see the roof so they called for backup. It looks as if it must have been driven down the slipway. It's sitting in about ten feet. We had to wait until the divers got here and they've just been down to confirm what it is.'

McBride was speaking quickly, his nervousness showing.

'And what is it, Sergeant?' Maxwell asked for confirmation.

'A Land Rover, sir.'

Maxwell exchanged a look with Gawn. Who is going to ask the next question, it seemed to say.

'Is there a body in it?' Gawn asked. It seemed she had been holding her breath for Maxwell could hear her expel a deep sigh on hearing the sergeant's reply.

'No, ma'am. The driver's window was open so either whoever was driving managed to get out before it sank or the body floated out and it's somewhere out there.'

McBride pointed out past the myriad of little islands seeming to float almost magically on the surface of the darkening water and on towards the western shores of the lough.

'So you haven't got a body yet?' she asked.

'No, ma'am. They're just about to get back into the water now. They'll have a look for a body but they say it would take a much larger-scale search if it's been carried further out. They're planning to hook the Land Rover up so the recovery vehicle can pull it out. They hope to have it done within the next half hour or so before it gets dark.'

'We'll wait.'

McBride's face showed what he thought of the DCI's words. No doubt he would have preferred not to have an audience for their work but he couldn't argue.

Gawn and Maxwell went back to his car and waited. Once or twice Maxwell made a desultory attempt at conversation but Gawn barely registered what he was saying so in the end he gave up. It was at times like this he wished he smoked. Then he would have had an excuse to get out of the car and away from her. She was making him even more anxious. He didn't like to think of the woman he had come to regard as a friend lying at the bottom of the lough.

Chapter 17

'They're bringing it up now.'

Maxwell had closed his eyes, just for a second. The tension in Gawn's voice had him immediately alert.

She was out of the car and halfway across the car park before he had caught her up. He glanced at her. He could sense the stress in her body. She was biting her lip, a mannerism he had noticed a few times before when she was under serious pressure. He noticed her hands were clenched into fists as they waited silently for the ghostly appearance of the vehicle.

They watched as the Land Rover was winched slowly out of the water and up the ramp, the whirr of the motor breaking the silence of the lough and the occasional screech of a bird flying past sounding almost like a scream of pain. Water was pouring off the bodywork and out of an open window as the car emerged, like a fairy-tale metal giant waking from its slumbers beneath the waves. Slowly. Clumsily. There was no obvious damage, no broken glass or dented bodywork, nothing to suggest a collision.

'Doesn't look as if there was an accident.' McBride gave his opinion although no one had asked for it. 'But that's quite a deceptive wee corner there and if it's dark and you don't know the road well and you're going a wee bit fast, well you can career off easy enough now.'

'And just manage to drive perfectly down the ramp?' Maxwell responded sceptically. He had walked over to the Land Rover and was looking through the open window. 'There's something on the passenger seat. A stain. Could be blood. Quite a lot of it, whatever it is.'

'We need to get it to Seapark right away.' Gawn had named the PSNI's forensic facility outside Carrickfergus. 'It'll have to be trailered there to preserve any evidence. Let them know, Paul. And tell them to make it a priority. If anybody questions that, you can tell them to speak to me.'

She turned to face the sergeant. 'You'll need to keep your people here until they can hand it over. Chain of evidence, Sergeant.'

'Yes, ma'am. Of course.'

His words said one thing, his face another. No doubt the encounter would add to her reputation as McBride would regale his colleagues with the story of his meeting with the famous Gawn Girvin, the targe. She didn't care.

Chapter 18

By the time they had negotiated their way through the traffic build-up around Newtownards and the always-busy Knock intersection on their way back to headquarters, evening was descending. Maxwell finally found the courage to ask the question.

'Do you think she's dead, Gawn?'

At first he thought she hadn't heard him, lost in her own thoughts. He was about to ask again when she spoke but her reply was hesitant.

'I don't know. I don't want to think that, but what's the alternative?'

He had driven through the security barrier and was pulling into a parking space before she spoke again. She swivelled round in the passenger seat to look directly at him.

'What are we saying? Jenny had a fight with Harri.' She saw his puzzled expression and explained. 'Harriet. Her friends called her Harri.'

A look of realisation spread across Maxwell's face.

'I heard her on the phone with someone called Harri last week,' he said. 'I was over at the Royal on the Maguire case and I called into her office for a chat. I caught the end of the call. It seemed a bit heated and I heard her calling the other person Harri. I thought it was a man.'

'That would have been Harriet. So, they argued on Monday night. We know that. But you don't kill someone because they won't take your advice, otherwise we'd be tripping over dead bodies all over the place.'

'*If* that's all it was. That's what she told you. If Jenny had been hoping to get together with her, she could have been angry if Harriet had just told her that she'd decided to get back with her husband. She could have lost her cool. It can happen to anybody. Maybe it was just a bit of pushing and shoving to start with. Girls' handbags stuff. And then Harriet trips or slips and bangs her head on the edge of the table. I'm not suggesting for a minute Jenny set out to kill her or even would have wanted to kill her when they were fighting.'

'So what are you suggesting, Paul? They fought and when Harri was hurt, instead of helping her, Jenny takes the opportunity to chase after her and hit her from behind with a rock? More than once? Does that sound like Jenny to you?'

'No. Of course not. But it does sound like a plausible scenario for a prosecution to paint.'

'If she did it, and I really cannot get my head round that, then she runs away, having the presence of mind to ditch her phone. It doesn't add up, Paul. Either she was angry and was acting on the spur of the moment or–'

'Well she's worked around police cases for years. She knows about tracking devices.'

'Then she drives down the Ards Peninsula – for whatever reason. I don't know if she has any associations with the area. She never mentioned any to me but that doesn't mean anything, and then she's overcome with remorse and drives off the slipway?'

She paused, waiting for his response.

'We don't really know Jenny that well. Not really. Maybe it wasn't suicide. Maybe she does have friends in the area. Maybe one of them helped her. It's just a pity the CCTV at the sailing club wasn't working. Someone might have met her there. Then they could have pushed the Land Rover into the water and she drove off with her friend, and she's hiding somewhere hoping everyone will assume she's drowned. She'll lie low for a while and then leave the country. We do know she's got friends in America. She could head back there.'

'I don't know if I prefer that scenario any better than the first. It's not much of a choice, is it?'

'Well, at least she'd still be alive.' Maxwell was trying to be encouraging.

Gawn seemed to give herself a shake. She pushed her hair back from her face. Maxwell waited to hear what she would say next.

'No. I won't believe it. Not Jenny.' She spoke and her voice sounded steely. He could imagine her addressing troops before an engagement. Whatever she was going to say, no one was going to contradict her. 'I want every traffic camera between Harriet's bungalow and the sailing club looked at.'

'There'll be a hell of a lot, boss. Think how many different ways she could have gone. It'll be a huge task.'

'Good. The more the better. It'll give us a better chance of picking something up on one of them somewhere.'

Maxwell could imagine the reaction when he ordered the team to trawl through all the footage. They'd moan about it. But not in front of her.

'We'll pull in some more bodies to help. I'll OK it and overtime too. As much as necessary. Send someone to travel the most likely routes. Whoever does it needs to get every bit of CCTV footage from buildings, including any security cameras from houses.'

What she was asking was huge, probably impossible. And she knew it.

'Is that what you think happened? Someone's taken her? God, Gawn, who? Not Hughes. Why would anybody take her?'

'I don't know. Yet. And I don't care how many hours it takes to find them on camera. They'll show up somewhere. Something should show up. Get it done.'

Her face was set. He knew it was useless to argue.

'McDowell won't be penny pinching on this one. He won't want the press getting on to a story about one of our own involved in a murder. Think of the headlines. Sensational stuff about sex triangles and God knows what. And that's before he knows anything about me. He'll approve extra staff and overtime. Anyhow, I'll handle him. I'm approving it.'

And, as he looked at her, he didn't doubt she would handle him. In her current mood, he reckoned even McDowell would think twice before contradicting her.

Chapter 19

Before she headed for home, Gawn wanted to call into the mortuary. Bad news travels fast and policemen are just as prone to gossiping as any other group of people, if not more so. Word would have already reached here of Jenny's involvement. She'd been surprised, but pleased, when

Maxwell had told her Munroe wanted to help. She needed his cooperation now.

'Chief Inspector, you're lucky you caught me. I was just about to leave. It's been a busy day what with one thing and another.' He didn't elaborate. 'I won't say nice to see you for the circumstances are most unfortunate, but it is good to know that you're on this case. For Dr Norris' sake.'

Professor Al Munroe, chief pathologist, had been on sabbatical since the Perfume Killer case, as the newspapers had called it. She had managed to keep all his embarrassing involvement out of the press and off the record and he had been very grateful to her for her discretion.

Now he stood facing her across his desk and continued in his soft Scottish lilt which often seemed so at odds with the human tragedies he was talking about.

'I gave Paul all the details of the PM. We're still waiting for a few more results but I don't think it's anything that would make a difference to your case.'

He held his hands out palms upwards as if he had nothing more to offer her.

'Thank you, Al. I appreciate you've been speedy on this one. I'm not here about the PM. I'm here to ask your permission to search Dr Norris' office. I didn't want to just barge in. I'd prefer it to be just between you and me and to do it myself. If I need to make it official and get the CSIs involved I will.' It was only a matter of time. Every second she could keep ahead of them might make all the difference to Jenny. 'For now, let's keep it under the radar. I don't really expect to find anything anyway.'

He nodded in agreement as she spoke.

'Of course. I understand. I know how discrete you can be, Chief Inspector. You're trying to protect Dr Norris' reputation. I can certainly relate to that. Go ahead. You know where it is.'

She turned to walk out of his office, and then, as an afterthought, turned back and voiced an idea which had just come to her.

'I haven't had a chance to read your full report yet. Paul filled me in on the time and cause of death, of course, but I have one question.'

'Yes?'

'Was there any sign of sexual activity?'

'Oh yes. There was. It's in the report. The victim had had sexual intercourse within the last few hours of her life.'

'Did you get a semen sample?'

'Yes. It's among the results we're waiting for. But there was no indication of any sexual assault and Maxwell didn't mention that you thought there'd been a sexual aspect to the murder.'

'We don't. But it all helps us get a picture of what went on in the hours before her death. If she was with someone and they had consensual sex it could change how we think about things.'

She turned and walked out.

Edward Hughes had visited his wife. They knew that. He had admitted it. Did they have sex while he was there? If so, by itself it proved nothing, except perhaps that he was telling the truth and they were going to get back together, which would only add to the suggestion that Jenny would have reacted angrily. Or had there been another man there after Hughes left? And was that before or after she herself had been there?

Could someone have been in the house with Harriet when she was outside? Was that why she hadn't answered the door? And when had Jenny gone back, if she had? Could she have been in the house too with Gawn outside? No. She would have noticed the Land Rover. She was sure there had been no other vehicles there except Harriet's own little red sports car.

If someone else had been there sometime later, who could that have been? Forensics had found no evidence of anyone else there… yet. But they hadn't finished their work. They were still searching the house. She was sure Damien Lyons would be especially thorough on this – his first crime scene in charge. But there were too many questions, too many uncertainties and too much circumstantial evidence pointing to Jenny Norris.

Chapter 20

Gawn paused outside the office door. She turned the handle. It wasn't locked. She put a pair of purple gloves on before walking in and turning on the main light switch. The evening had closed in now and the sky outside was black, the window reflecting back her own worried image. She could see lights twinkling from hundreds of windows in the main building across the hospital complex.

Everything was just as the pathologist must have left it on Friday. Gawn noticed a painting on the wall behind the desk. She was sure it had not been there the last time she had visited Jenny here. It was a watercolour of Slieve Donard. She recognised the famous peak and recognised the signature of the artist too – HH.

The objects on the desk – a telephone, notepad and pen, a desk diary, and an old Boston Celtics mug with a broken handle being employed as a pen and pencil holder – sat in perfect symmetry, evidence of Jenny's OCD tendencies that Gawn teased her friend about. She lifted the diary and flicked through it. She noted the cryptic entry for Monday – GG Dub 8CS – their arrangements to travel to Dublin on the eight o'clock Enterprise train leaving Central Station for her day at the clinic. Then she turned her attention to the notepad.

The top page was blank but an earlier page had been ripped out leaving a thin line of serrated paper along the top to evidence its existence. She was tempted to deploy the old trick with a pencil to bring up the indentations but knew Mark Ferguson or whoever eventually would be organising the search here would be livid if she messed with their evidence. She needed to leave no trace of her search.

Gawn sat down at the desk and opened first one drawer, then the other. There was nothing surprising or revealing. Some folders of reports Jenny must have been working on, a box of paper clips, more pens, a packet of paper hankies, some mints, a bottle of paracetamol tablets, a little jar of a menthol rub which Gawn knew the pathologist offered sometimes to visiting police officers witnessing her work with a particularly pungent cadaver, and a tube of cough lozenges.

Gawn was just about to close the drawer when she glimpsed the edge of a piece of pink paper right in the very back corner almost jammed into the joint in the wood. It had been folded over into a tiny square. She lifted it out carefully and flattened it out so she could read what was written on it. There was an address in Newcastle, County Down, at the top of the page. It was a receipt for a deposit on a rental property in the seaside town nestled at the foot of the Mournes. The date on it was just last week and the rental was for three months beginning last Friday.

Why had Jenny been renting a property in Newcastle? She had only recently bought her apartment in the old bakery complex in South Belfast. Then it dawned on her that Newcastle was Mourne country, one of Jenny's favourite boltholes. Perhaps she planned to do a lot of hill walking. But was it just for herself? Maybe this was proof that she and Harri were in some more committed relationship or maybe she was just jumping to conclusions again. They would need to check it out.

Then another thought struck her. Maybe Jenny was hiding there now. Gawn decided to say nothing about her find to anyone. Not even Maxwell. If she could find Jenny herself quickly and quietly and bring her back, they might be able to get her involvement sorted out and then go after the real killer.

She put the folded paper back in the drawer exactly as she had found it ready to be discovered by a CSI when they eventually would be summoned to search. This new information gave her a head start. She would drive to Newcastle first thing in the morning. With luck, she'd find Jenny and they'd be able to sort it all out.

She didn't really believe that but she had to hope.

Chapter 21

Gawn texted Maxwell the next morning to explain she had a call to make and wouldn't be there for the morning briefing. She gave him no details about where she was going or what she was doing. He texted back almost immediately that Mark Ferguson wanted to see her urgently. The crime scene manager had phoned and he had sounded angry. She hoped it meant his team had found something useful at Jenny's apartment. She feared it meant that he had found out she'd already been there and searched the place. She asked Maxwell to arrange a time for him to see her in the afternoon.

Gawn had then set out in heavy traffic heading onto the M2 into Belfast. When she had cleared the city and was wending her way up the Saintfield Road, the congestion started to ease, and she allowed herself some time to speculate on what she hoped or feared she would find at the end of her journey. Best case, she would find Jenny with a simple explanation for her disappearance and her car ending up in Strangford Lough although she couldn't think what on earth it could be. Worst case, she would get it confirmed that Jenny and Harri had planned to set up home together, giving her the perfect reason to lose her temper if Harri had betrayed her with her husband or some other mystery man.

Soon the magnificent Mourne Mountains came into view. At this time of year low clouds draped themselves over the slopes like a grey fleecy shawl slung over the shoulders of an elderly grande dame. Gawn couldn't help thinking of happy holidays she and her family had spent in some of the caravan parks here.

The one-way traffic system in Newcastle took her along the seafront until she could turn off and head to the address she had carefully put into her sat nav before setting out. The receipt had been for the let of a property called French's Cottage, no doubt a lure to foreign tourists, fans of Percy French, composer of the world-famous song *The Mountains of Mourne*. But it hadn't given details of exactly where the cottage was and an internet search had turned up no property of that name. She was heading to the address on the receipt, hoping someone there would be able to tell her.

Number ten Sheskin Mount was an older red-brick detached house in a residential area on the edge of town well away from the amusement arcades, the boating park and the friendly cafés and fish and chip shops which lined the main street and were so beloved by day trippers. It looked as if it had seen better days, with window frames clearly in need of a coat of paint and a gravel driveway that was more weeds than gravel, but she was pleased to see a car parked outside. Hopefully this meant someone was at home to direct her to French's Cottage.

Gawn approached the front door. She wasn't sure who or what she expected when she knocked. The door opened but only wide enough to let a middle-aged woman, with greying hair scraped back from her face in a ponytail, look out, leaving the security chain still firmly in place.

'Yes?'

The one word was filled with suspicion. The woman was giving nothing away. There was no greeting, no welcoming smile. For a holiday resort and an area famed for its warm welcome to tourists, Gawn was surprised. She didn't think she looked like a typical hawker in her smart business suit or part of some sort of scam, but she supposed you could never tell these days and the PSNI was always warning older people to be suspicious when strangers called unexpectedly.

'Good morning. I'm sorry to disturb you so early, madam.' She was only now realising it was barely nine o'clock. Perhaps a little early to be making a call unannounced? She hadn't considered that, focused only on finding Jenny Norris as quickly as possible.

Gawn smiled in what she hoped was an encouraging way, wanting to allay the woman's concerns.

'I'm DCI Girvin of the Serious Crimes Squad.'

She held up her ID and was surprised to see the woman scrutinising it carefully, her eyes moving from the photograph to Gawn's face and back again. Usually people accepted, once a card was produced, that you were who you said you were. This woman still seemed wary.

'Yes?'

'May I come in?'

'What's it about?'

The door was still only just ajar so Gawn could only see half of the woman's face. But she was puzzled why she was getting such a frosty reception. Why was the woman so suspicious? For one minute the thought came into her mind that perhaps Jenny was hiding here, had seen her arriving and had told the woman to get rid of her.

'I'm inquiring about a property in this area – French's Cottage. I believe a friend of mine has rented it and I wanted to find out exactly where it is.'

'Who's your friend?'

'Her name's Jenny Norris.'

The door was slammed in her face.

Chapter 22

Gawn jumped back in surprise. Then she heard the metallic jingling of the security chain being slid across and the door swung wide open. The woman, who looked a little older now Gawn could see all of her, stood squarely in front of her, dressed in a pair of faded jeans and an oversized bright green jumper which reached down almost to her knees. She was smiling broadly now. No sign of the earlier suspicion. Gawn could see that her greying hair was held back by a green velvet scrunchie and she noted the deep wrinkles by the sides of her eyes, laughter lines.

'You're the famous Gawn. Jenny's told us all about you. She said if we ever needed help we could trust you. Come in! Come in!'

The woman seemed to have gone from one extreme to the other. Now she was welcoming her in like the prodigal son. She took Gawn's hand and shook it, pumping it up and down enthusiastically, seeming like she was never going to let it go. Then she closed the front door behind them and Gawn noticed she put the safety chain carefully back in place.

'Come away in, dear.'

She led the policewoman up a wide hallway holding her by the elbow and guiding her as if she was a child. They walked into a high-ceilinged room at the back of the house which was obviously the kitchen. A large saucepan of something delicious was simmering on a huge range cooker. The smell of coffee reached Gawn's nostrils too and she breathed in deeply. Usually by this time in the morning she was on her second or third cup. Two women, one with a baby sucking at her breast, were sitting at the table. They looked up at her and smiled shyly, then quickly looked away again and resumed their whispered conversation.

'Coffee, dear?'

Gawn was surprised that she was now being treated like an honoured guest or maybe more like an old friend and felt as if she was losing control of the situation. She was here to ask questions and find answers. Instead she was finding more mysteries. Who were these women and what was going on?

'Yes, thank you,' was all she could manage to say.

'Jenny told us how much you like your coffee.'

The woman lifted a cafetière and poured the contents into a Boston Celtics mug, a match for the one in Jenny's office, only this one still had its handle. Steam rose from the mug and the fragrant aroma of the freshly ground coffee filled the air.

'Just made. You timed your arrival perfectly. And black. Jenny told us you take it black, no milk, no sugar. We'll let you use Jenny's mug since she's not here today.'

It was obvious this woman knew nothing about the events of the last two days or that Jenny Norris was in trouble.

'Mrs…' Gawn began and then stopped. She didn't even know who she was speaking to.

'Ach, sorry. Where are my manners? I'm Tilly, Tilly Mulligan. And this is Tracey and Janine. Not their real names,' she added in a conspiratorial stage whisper.

Why did they need different names? Gawn had already realised, from their muted conversation when she'd first walked into the kitchen, that the women were foreign. She guessed, probably Polish or Romanian, definitely somewhere in eastern Europe. The baby had finished feeding now and had been hoisted over her mother's shoulder to be winded. The tiny girl – if the little pink cardigan was to be a guide – gave a few mewling cries as the young mother patted her gently on the back. Gawn couldn't help herself watching, fascinated, as the baby worked her chubby little fingers clutching at the air and her mother's hair. Gawn had never really had much to do with babies. Nothing really. It was a closed world to her, a mysterious land of smelly nappies and teething and sleepless nights; a world she had listened to others talking about; a world she wasn't yet totally sure she was ready to be a part of.

She pulled her thoughts back to the present and the reason for her visit.

'Tilly, I'm afraid I'm at a bit of a disadvantage here. You might know all about me.' She hoped she certainly didn't. 'But Jenny's never mentioned anything about you or this place to me.'

'You know, I wondered if she would have told you about us. I know you're her friend but I suppose it's better the fewer people who know about us and sometimes we do have to bend the rules a wee bit. She might have thought that might put you in a difficult position, you being in the police and all.'

'Know what about you?'

'That this is a refuge for women who need to get away, to escape, to run away from the men who are abusing them. Some of them are battered wives and some are victims of people smuggling or prostitution rings.' Her eyes moved to the two young women across the room for a split second and then back to Gawn. 'We get them away from their partners or pimps but we have to keep our work very quiet, very secret. We don't want any husbands or partners or worse arriving up at the door and scaring the women and children trying to get in.'

Gawn couldn't help herself. She glanced across at the two women who looked back at her. She saw now that their eyes were sad and frightened in spite of their shy smiles and she noticed the scarring on the arm of one of the women. It looked like a neat row of cigarette burns.

'I found a receipt for French's Cottage. I had no idea about this place or that Jenny was involved in anything like this.'

'Oh, she's one of our main supporters. She's got us a lot of money and help from voluntary bodies and friends of hers in America and she dips into her own pockets when we're short. She's a saint. That's what the receipts are for. We've had more women than usual coming to us over the last few weeks and money was a bit tight. There's no such place as French's Cottage but when Jenny or any of our other supporters make a donation it means there's no paper trail to us as a refuge. It looks just like a business transaction, like they're renting a place for a week or something.'

Gawn didn't really understand why receipts were necessary, why someone couldn't just give a donation. It was probably something to do with tax or charitable status or something like that. But, whatever the reason, it wasn't important. She was finding out something new about her friend. She had never thought of her in quite this light before. A saint? Kind, generous, caring, supportive. Yes. She shouldn't really be surprised. After all Jenny had given up her day off to be with her on Monday when Seb couldn't be there. Jenny's presence had turned what could have been an ordeal into something at least bearable. Was this the person who had chased Harriet Hughes and bashed her head in with a rock? Of course not.

Jenny had told Tilly she could trust her. Now Gawn was going to trust Tilly too.

'Jenny's in trouble.'

The older woman's smile faded instantly when she heard those words.

'She's disappeared and her Land Rover was found yesterday in Strangford Lough.'

The woman's face had grown paler.

'*In* the lough? You think she's dead?' Tilly was shaking her head in disbelief. 'You think she committed suicide? No, you don't because then you wouldn't be here looking for her, would you?'

'The Jenny I know wouldn't commit suicide,' Gawn replied, 'but we're looking for her because we suspect she was on the scene when a woman was battered to death, so she's a person of interest in our inquiries. We're looking for her to question her about that and we think she may have dumped the car in the lough and is hiding somewhere.'

Tilly's mouth had fallen further and further open as Gawn had been speaking.

'You think Jenny Norris killed somebody? And you think she's here, don't you?' There was a flash of anger in her eyes.

'I didn't even know about this place until yesterday. I came here because I found a receipt for French's Cottage and I wanted to check if she was hiding there. So, if there is no French's Cottage…'

Gawn didn't finish her sentence, just waited for a response.

'You want to know if she's hiding here?'

The woman stood up. Gawn stood too. Although Tilly was easily six inches shorter than her and probably nearly twenty years older too, she had quite a formidable appearance when she drew herself up to her full height. Gawn reckoned she would have had to develop a tough persona to do the kind of work she did and face up to some of the people she would have come across.

'Yes. If she is, I want to help her. I'd have to take her in for questioning but I promise I'll find the truth.'

Seconds ticked by while Tilly seemed to be making up her mind what she would say next.

'You want the truth?' she asked.

'Of course.'

'She's not here but, to be honest with you, the truth, I wouldn't tell you if she was. No way would Jenny be involved in killing anybody. You should know that too, Gawn Girvin. Shame on you! You're meant to be her friend. Who's she supposed to have killed anyway?'

'A woman called Harriet Hughes.'

She saw a look of recognition cross Tilly's face.

'You've heard of her?'

'Jenny brought her here a couple of weeks ago. They were down in Newcastle walking in the Mournes and she called in. She wanted Harri to know there was somewhere she could go if anything happened.'

'You can't expect me just to take your word for it that Jenny's not here. This is a murder inquiry, Tilly.'

'We'll not be having the police in here searching. These women have already been terrorised and brutalised by men, some of them policemen in their own countries. You'll need a search warrant and we'll fight it tooth and nail. I'll be on to my local MLA as soon as you go.'

Gawn didn't believe that Jenny was hiding here. Tilly wasn't such a good actress. She hadn't known anything about what had happened. It had come as a shock to her. That was obvious. She hoped that if Jenny had been in the house, she would have revealed herself by now anyway and talked to her.

'I won't be getting a search warrant, Tilly. At least not yet and not unless it's absolutely necessary. But if Jenny does contact you, please tell her to get in touch with me. I can't help her if she keeps running.'

She searched around in her handbag and drew out a business card which she set down on the table along with several banknotes, all the cash she had with her.

'She knows my number anyway but now you have it too. If there's anything you can tell me to help, ring me. Any time.'

As she was walking towards the front door, Tilly's parting words stopped her.

'There were men threatening her. Have you looked into that?'

Gawn swung round to face the other woman again.

'What men?'

'She helped some girls to escape from a gang, I think. I know she thought she was being followed and she'd had a few strange phone calls. She didn't give me any details but she told me she was being careful.'

Suddenly Jenny's disappearance became more complicated and the chances of finding her alive more distant.

Chapter 23

'So you're saying Jenny could be hiding out from gang members or an angry husband because of her association with this women's group? Or that somebody grabbed her because of that and is holding her somewhere?'

Gawn had returned from her trip to Newcastle and immediately called Maxwell into her office.

'I'm saying it's just something more to add to the list of possibilities. As if the list wasn't long enough already. If someone had been following her, as she seems to have suspected according to Tilly, they could have killed Harri and then grabbed her to stop her talking.'

'And done what with her? If they'd already killed Harri, why not just kill Jenny too?' He almost added 'two birds with one stone' but realised it would sound totally callous and Gawn would probably go ballistic at him.

'I don't know, Paul.'

She was sitting down now and she ran her fingers through her hair pushing it back off her face in exasperation. Maxwell caught a glimpse of a scar at her hairline. He knew she'd been injured in Afghanistan but she never talked about it; never talked about her time in the army at all. She looked pale. She had been looking strained all week ever since her day off on Monday.

'It's all just getting murkier by the minute. We need facts. We need to know if she was being followed and who it was who was phoning her. Have they finished with her phone yet?'

'No. I think they're still working on it.'

'Put a bit of pressure on them. No. Put a *lot* of pressure on them. If they give you any guff, let me know and I'll talk to them myself. We don't want to waste time going up dead-ends. If she was getting threatening phone calls they should be able to trace them. What about the CCTV footage? Any luck with it?'

He shook his head.

'ANPR pick up anything?'

Another shake of his head.

'Nothing turn up with any of the interviews?'

'Nothing yet.'

'She can't just have disappeared into thin air. She couldn't dematerialise at the bungalow and suddenly reappear in Strangford to ditch her car. She has to show up somewhere.' Gawn sounded exasperated.

Maxwell could see how edgy she was getting.

'What about Ms Bingham? Did anyone check her whereabouts on Monday night?' she asked.

'Cast-iron alibi, I'm afraid. She was at some big legal "do" in London. She even had her photograph taken with the Lord Chief Justice. Flew back first thing on Tuesday morning. And there's something else.'

'Yes?'

'They got the DNA results from the swabs the duty doctor took. The scrape on Hughes' arm wasn't a match for his wife. We don't have Natalie Bingham's DNA but now we know for sure it couldn't have been her.'

'So we suspect Hughes was with another woman on Monday night. Right.'

Gawn stood up abruptly.

'Let's go and talk to him. He knows more than he's told us. I want to know how Harri was involved in his business. It all sounds iffy to me. I wonder if he's at home.'

'He's not.'

'How do you know?'

'I put him under surveillance. I thought if he was involved and he had grabbed Jenny or knew where she is, then he might lead us to her.'

He could see Gawn was pleased. She would be annoyed at herself for not having thought of it, he suspected.

'This morning he went into the office.'

'Any visitors?'

'Only Ms Bingham last night.'

'Surprise, surprise. Comforting the grieving husband. She may not have been with him on Monday night but she's moving in on him now. Let's talk to him.'

'Don't forget you have Mark coming in to see you at three,' he said.

He knew she wouldn't have forgotten and she'd be expecting it to be a difficult meeting. Her face betrayed she wasn't looking forward to it.

Chapter 24

Altor Pharmaceuticals was on an industrial estate on the outskirts of North Belfast but they had trouble finding it hidden away down a warren of streets of little back-to-back houses. Somehow, from the name and their website,

Gawn had expected large-scale factory premises and expansive offices, lots of steel and glass, a symbol of modernity and innovation. Instead, they found themselves outside a single-storey grey block building, featureless and looking more like a warehouse than a state-of-the-art facility. Only a few vehicles sat in a row in the car park in front of it. A large sign in red letters proclaimed 'Altor Pharmaceuticals' and an arrow directed them to a single glass door.

'What do they actually do here again, Paul?'

'They're a centre for research, according to their website. They provide support for partner companies to develop new drugs and treatments. I would assume it's another case of the government pouring a lot of money into some company to attract them to set up and provide jobs for locals and use our well-educated workforce to make profits for themselves. Then when the grants run out, they take off.'

Gawn noted more than a little hint of cynicism in his voice.

'Billy said they're partnered with a company called Eureka Advances in San Francisco. It boasts that they're working on various tests to detect cancers at an early stage. It sounds great. Their website's glossy and professional-looking. But their work is shrouded in secrecy in case one of their competitors beats them to it, I suppose.'

Maxwell finished what he was saying and pushed the bell. A disembodied female voice with a broad Belfast accent responded almost immediately.

'Yes? Can I help you?'

They could see a camera mounted over the door and Gawn held up her ID to it as she spoke.

'DCI Girvin and DI Maxwell, PSNI. Here to see Edward Hughes.'

They didn't have an appointment. She had decided to surprise him. Anyhow, if they'd rung ahead Hughes might have refused to see them. Turning up unexpectedly would put him under more pressure.

The buzzer sounded and the door catch was released, allowing them to walk in. Directly in front of them was a reception desk and the voice spoke again, but this time accompanied by a friendly smile from a mousy-looking young woman.

'I'll let Dr Hughes know you're here. Did he know you were coming? You're not in the diary.'

'No,' Gawn replied.

'Well, if you'd just like to take a seat, please.'

She motioned to a row of hard plastic chairs ranged tightly against the wall rather like a doctor's waiting room. Gawn's mind immediately went to Monday and her experiences in Dublin. There had been a lot of sitting around waiting on hard chairs involved in that visit too.

But they didn't have to wait very long this time. Within a few minutes Hughes appeared through a set of double doors. He didn't look pleased to see them. In fact he looked furious but as he approached the two detectives they could see he was struggling to disguise his annoyance.

'What is it now? I thought I'd told you all I know. Mr Hartnett says I'm not to answer any more questions without him being with me. He says you can't harass me.'

He was trying to keep his voice even and low and he glanced at the receptionist as he spoke. She was paying them no heed, her head buried in a magazine.

'We certainly have no intention of harassing you, Dr Hughes. We just thought, seeing you were well enough to come back to work, you might feel able to help with our inquiries a bit more. To find your wife's killer. It's just a few background questions, sir. Just a wee chat. Nothing about finding your wife's body,' Gawn assured him. 'We need to understand your wife's involvement in your company.'

As soon as she mentioned this, Hughes took a step towards them and it seemed as if he was going to take her forcibly by the arm, then thought better of it. He was still only inches away from her as he spoke and Maxwell had tensed ready to spring into action if the man made any move against her.

'Not here. I'll talk to you in my office.'

He almost hissed the words at them, his eyes flashing with barely controlled rage. This was the Edward Hughes she wanted to see, a man capable of anger and violence.

He swung round and started to walk away. As Gawn had suspected, whatever Hughes was planning, he did not want his employers to know. She couldn't imagine that they'd be pleased to lose him when there might be the possibility of him taking some of his research with him. Drug treatments and breakthroughs could be worth millions. If Hughes had made some major discovery, Altor would want to benefit from it.

As they watched him walking away, they realised they were expected to follow. The girl at reception lifted her head out of her magazine as they passed but then quickly went back to the article she was reading about the latest drama in the life of some Hollywood actor, with no further interest in the real-life drama that was happening in front of her.

Hughes' office was at the end of a long corridor decorated with sepia prints of famous scenes from around the world, the Eiffel Tower, the Golden Gate Bridge, the Sydney Opera House, the Terracotta Warriors. Gawn wondered what any of these places had to do with Altor and decided it was simply an attempt to create the image of an international company.

While the appearance of the building had been less than impressive, Hughes' office was very different. Gawn's first thought was that it was like something from a Bond movie. An expensive-looking glass desk and heavy leather revolving chair faced the door.

One wall held a bank of computers, another was covered with notes and diagrams, coloured pages and all kinds of numbers and figures which must mean something to their suspect. A set of low bookshelves held a range of files, their covers bringing a touch of colour to the otherwise monochrome room, a masculine domain. Framed diplomas hung on the wall over the shelves and some personal items were sitting out including some framed photographs.

Gawn was surprised to see some baby pictures on display. The Hughes didn't have any children. Her gaze took the whole room in without pausing. The overall impression of the space was organised, business-like but with some homely touches which surprised her.

Before she had time to speak, Hughes jumped in keen to close down any questions.

'I can't discuss my personal business here. The fact that I'm starting up my own company is very sensitive information.' His voice was low, not quite a whisper but not much louder, and he was agitated. He kept glancing at the door as if he was afraid someone would come in and hear them. 'It's at a very crucial point. I'm about to make my move but I need to sort the last few bits and pieces out.'

'Like getting your wife to sign whatever you brought to her on Monday night?' Maxwell prompted.

'Yes. I needed her to sign to allow me to remortgage our home,' he reluctantly agreed.

'And she wouldn't?' Gawn asked.

'No. She agreed.'

'Was that before or after you had sex with her?'

Maxwell looked shocked at the question but Hughes was outraged. His mouth opened in surprise but then he recovered and gave her a withering look.

'I didn't realise it was a crime to have sex with your wife. What are you now, the morality police?'

'We're just trying to find your wife's killer. The mood she was in and what happened to her prior to her murder are all relevant to our investigation.'

Hughes glared at her.

'Why did you go back on Tuesday morning, sir?' Maxwell said, trying to move things on.

Hughes' expression was thunderous. He was seething and the DCI wasn't much better.

'I'd left something behind and I needed it urgently.'

'What? The mortgage papers?' Maxwell asked.

'No.'

He hesitated and both detectives were aware of a guardedness coming over his face. Whatever it was, Hughes didn't want to tell them. So they just waited. The silence grew but Gawn knew that Hughes would break first, so long as Maxwell didn't say anything. Reluctantly, Hughes spoke.

'If you must know, it was a blood sample.'

'A blood sample.' It was Maxwell who repeated his words. 'You'd taken a blood sample to your wife's and then left it behind?'

'It was a sample of my wife's blood. And that's all I'm prepared to say. It has nothing to do with your investigation. It won't help you find who killed her. Now, if you have any other questions, direct them to my solicitor.'

* * *

'So now we have Count Dracula as a suspect. People are freakin' weird.'

Maxwell was climbing into the passenger seat and Gawn had already put the car into reverse and was just about to drive out of the car park.

'You're not only realising that now, Paul? Did they find a vial of blood in the bungalow?'

'I don't know. I didn't look through everything they listed. I think I might have noticed that but maybe not. Why? What are you thinking?'

'Well, if it's there, we should get it tested. Make sure it is Harriet's blood. Verify that part of his story. Hughes needed it for something and it wasn't for her to sign her name in blood on the mortgage.' It was the nearest she had got to a joke in the last three days. 'If it isn't there then either he lied about what he came back for or he lied and he was inside on Tuesday morning and got it.'

'Or someone else took it.' Maxwell finished her thoughts.

'Still too many possibilities, Paul. We need to catch a break.'

She accelerated away.

Chapter 25

The phone on her desk was ringing as Gawn walked into her office.

'Girvin.'

'Gawn, it's Robert Boyd. I got the message that you wanted to speak to me. My sergeant explained what it was about.'

Gawn recognised the deep voice of her counterpart in the Public Protection Branch. DCI Robert Boyd headed up a unit which dealt with domestic and child abuse cases, sexual exploitation, rape and child abuse imagery, which was becoming a very big issue. She had nothing but admiration for him and his team. She knew she could never do the work they did. She had had a taste of it in a previous case. Some of the things she had witnessed then would stay with her forever.

'Thanks for calling me back, Robert. Have you got anything to help me?' She was clutching the phone under her chin while she removed her jacket and sat down behind her desk. She slipped off her shoes and got comfortable in her chair as he started speaking.

'There are various organised groups bringing women into the country from eastern Europe. They sometimes use violence, but it's mostly against their competitors or their women if they're not compliant. I haven't heard of them going after any outsiders. But I wouldn't rule it out completely.

'I have heard of your French's Cottage group in Newcastle too. They don't publicise their work. It's very much word of mouth stuff and they don't involve us basically because I think they mightn't totally stay within the law. I have no hard evidence of that, mind. It's just that often our hands are tied and Social Services have so many regulations to deal with and so many hoops to jump through before they can act that we can't do as much as we'd like to or act as quickly as we want. Plus we have to look at the bigger picture. We want to go after the bosses, shut down the organisations, not necessarily stop the wee man running a couple of prostitutes or giving his partner a slap the odd Saturday night when he's had a few too many.'

He heard her sharp intake of breath and realised he better explain himself.

'I know that sounds harsh, Gawn. And I'm not minimising domestic violence. Believe me, I've seen enough of it, more than enough. If I could, I would get every last one of them and lock them up and throw away the key, but you can't save everybody. It's just not possible. We don't have the resources and when we close one lot down another lot pops up somewhere else. It's like whack-a-mole and it's big business. Lucrative. And less dangerous for them than running drugs where they come up against the paramilitaries. This French's Cottage lot goes straight for it when someone comes to them for help and just ignores everything else.'

'Which is all well and good when it works,' Gawn interjected.

'For them, yes, but it can bugger up months of surveillance and undercover work for us.'

She could hear the frustration in his voice. 'So they're not your favourite people, Robert.'

'I wouldn't say that exactly. I understand why they do what they do. I admire their motives. I don't condone any violence against women. I have two teenage daughters myself but sometimes we have to stay back. It's the only way to get to the big fish. The greater good, Gawn.'

Gawn had had that argument of the greater good served up to her before both in the army and in the police. She understood it but she didn't like it.

'So, Robert, in short, you don't think it's likely that Dr Norris was being followed by any of your criminal groups.'

'I didn't say that. It's possible. I've no way of knowing. She could have rattled someone's cage. With a few of these men that doesn't take very much but to be honest with you, Gawn, I don't see what they would gain from taking her and holding her somewhere. Roughing her up, threatening her to scare her off, maybe even killing her, but kidnapping her? It would just bring more heat down on them. And, if they had killed her, I don't see them taking the time to hide her body. You'd have found her by now.'

She thought he was probably right. The fact that Jenny's body hadn't turned up yet offered her some hope that her friend was still alive.

'Thanks, Robert. At least I can put this further down my list of possibilities and concentrate on some of the others.'

She wasn't particularly comforted by what he had said. If someone had been following Jenny, if she had crossed traffickers or some gang, then it seemed more likely she would be dead than being held somewhere and they just hadn't found her body yet.

'If I hear anything, I'll let you know. I'll ask around. Good luck, Gawn. I hope you find her. I've worked with

Jenny Norris a few times. She's dead on for a pathologist.' And then he laughed at his own pun. 'Sorry. I couldn't resist it. Good luck.' And he rang off.

Boyd's comments hadn't really helped her. She agreed with him that it seemed unlikely Jenny had been followed by someone connected with the women from French's Cottage. But a violent husband, a possible sex triangle, industrial espionage, Hughes up to no good with blood samples and even the battered women. She had too many possible motives and too many suspects and to any outsider, Jenny would still be top of the list. Not her list.

Chapter 26

It was almost three in the afternoon and she couldn't concentrate on anything. There were reports sitting on her desk but Gawn hadn't even glanced at them. She was preparing herself for Ferguson's visit. She wasn't looking forward to it. She knew she had been in the wrong searching Jenny's apartment and her office – which he couldn't even know about yet – but she didn't regret doing it. And she would do it again. She just didn't look forward to explaining herself to the CSM.

When her phone rang, she jumped. Her nerves were frayed.

'Girvin.'

'There's a Mrs Lattimer on the phone wanting to speak to you, ma'am.'

For a second she couldn't place the name. Then she remembered Jenny's brother-in-law was Nigel Lattimer, the MLA. This must be Jenny's sister, Melanie.

'Put her through.'

There was the slightest pause and then a woman's hesitant voice came on the line.

'Chief Inspector Girvin?'

'Yes. I'm Gawn Girvin and you're Jenny's sister.'

'Yes. My mother told me you'd visited her yesterday and she gave me your number. I hope it's alright phoning you like this.'

'Of course, Mrs Lattimer. How can I help you?' What she really wanted to ask was how could the woman help her.

'Is my sister in some sort of trouble?'

Gawn's heart sank. Unless this was a double bluff that Jenny had put her sister up to, to check how far the search for her had progressed, then this woman knew nothing.

'When was the last time you saw your sister?'

'Last week. We had coffee together last Tuesday and we spoke on the phone on Sunday night. She told me she was going to Dublin with you on Monday.'

Gawn hoped Jenny hadn't told her why they were going.

'She was looking forward to hitting the shops in Grafton Street. But I haven't heard from her since and she isn't answering her phone. I'd expected her to ring and tell me what she'd bought. Something's wrong, isn't it?'

Gawn had a decision to make. How much should she tell Melanie Lattimer? It was not public knowledge that they were searching for Jenny nor that she was a person of interest in the inquiry. Harriet's murder had attracted some publicity but with a major industrial dispute going on that was affecting oil supplies and a missing teenage girl on the front pages of the papers, there hadn't been too much press coverage yet.

'I haven't seen Jenny since Monday. She isn't at her apartment and we're concerned for her safety. It's very important that she contact us as soon as possible so we know she's alright. I simply wanted your parents to let me know if she turned up at their house.'

There was a noise which sounded like a snort on the end of the line.

'Little chance of that.'

'Then I'll ask you what I asked them. If she gets in touch with you, please let me know right away.'

'Of course. But if you hear from her, I expect you to let me know, Chief Inspector.'

'That seems fair.'

Melanie Lattimer rang off. Gawn hadn't learned anything new but the phone call had encouraged her. At least someone in her family cared about Jenny.

Chapter 27

The knock on Gawn's office door sounded angry. If knocks can sound angry, she thought. It was exactly 3pm and she knew it would be Mark Ferguson. She had asked Maxwell to keep away and keep everyone else away too; to make sure she wasn't disturbed. She needed to clear the air with the crime scene manager. Gawn had nothing but respect for his work and she didn't want to lose the good working relationship they'd had up to now, but she expected he would pull no punches in telling her exactly what he thought of what she had done at Jenny's apartment and he didn't even know about her searching the office yet.

She sat up a little straighter in her chair and took a deep breath and blew out her cheeks before responding.

'Come.'

The door opened and Ferguson walked in. She had never seen him scowling before. He invariably had a smile on his face no matter how unpleasant or gruesome the circumstances of their meeting.

'Mark, sit down.'

'I'd prefer to stand.'

And he stood there, in front of her desk, facing her. His back was rigid and he didn't take his eyes off her face. It was a confrontational stance. It was like a competition of staring each other out that she hadn't played since the school playground.

'And I'd prefer you to sit.'

Her voice was quiet and controlled. Standing, he towered over her at her desk. She looked up at him and their eyes locked. If confrontation was what he wanted, she could oblige. The way she was feeling right now with this case, she'd welcome the opportunity to let off a bit of steam at someone. She knew she was in the wrong but she was prepared to take him on. It would be a relief to feel something other than the powerlessness she was feeling at their lack of progress.

For just a few seconds it was a battle of wills but a battle only she could win. Her words hadn't exactly been an order, more an invitation, but if he didn't sit then she would order him to. He hesitated and then he seemed to think better of it and sat down.

No point in playing games. She decided to get straight to the point.

'You know I'd already looked around Dr Norris' apartment before you did, don't you?'

Ferguson didn't reply. She could see the muscles at the side of his jaw contracting where he was clenching his teeth. She could imagine what he would like to say to her.

Having to justify herself was not something she was used to; yet, in all fairness to Ferguson, she felt he deserved some sort of an explanation. She didn't want him thinking she didn't trust his work.

'Look, Mark, when I went there, I was looking for Dr Norris. Just that. I didn't go there to search the apartment.'

That wasn't totally true, of course. She hadn't wanted to wait to get the paperwork together for his team to be able to carry out a search.

'I thought it was possible she might be ill or something had happened to her and she could be lying unconscious on the floor. She wasn't answering her phone.' She thought she sounded as if she was making excuses and, of course, she was. 'Once I was inside, it seemed stupid not to use the opportunity to look for something to help me find her.'

Ferguson still didn't make any comment. The silent treatment. So that was the way he was going to play it. Not quite insolence but he wasn't going to make it easy for her either.

'I touched as little as possible, Mark, and I was wearing gloves the whole time. I didn't interfere or contaminate the scene and I wasn't even sure when I was there that it was a crime scene. I'm still not sure. Dr Norris might simply have left in a hurry. And left a mess behind her.'

'It is a crime scene.' He spoke with certainty.

'What did you find?' She leant towards him, excited, eager to hear what he had to say.

'Someone, other than you, had been in there looking around.'

'But I checked the lock. It hadn't been forced. I couldn't see any marks of tampering on it.'

'That's because he didn't break in. He used a key.'

'How did he…' she began and then answered her own question. 'He had Jenny's key, of course.' Which means he had Jenny or someone had Jenny or… her mind was racing through a combination of circumstances and their implications. Had Jenny been forced to give her key up? Had she been in a position to refuse to give her key up or was she already dead and her key taken from her? But why? What were they looking for?

'That would seem to be the most logical answer. The neighbour certainly hadn't loaned him hers as she did with you.'

Gawn chose to ignore Ferguson's pointed comment and asked, 'But how do you know someone else was there if there was no forced entry?'

'Two things. We found a set of fingerprints.'

'Where?'

'On a cardboard box.'

Gawn remembered the empty box sitting in Jenny's lounge.

'Our man carried it in. It was his excuse for being there in the building. He was a delivery man ostensibly,' he explained. 'We checked the CCTV. There are no cameras in the corridors but there is one in the front lobby at the entrance to the building and one in the lift and we have him entering around 7.30 on Tuesday morning carrying a package and going up to the top floor.'

'So, round about the time when the body of Harriet Hughes was found?'

'Yes. He'd used gloves, like yourself.' He paused for just a split second, seeming to want to reinforce his unspoken criticism of her actions. 'Inside the apartment. He's a pro but he'd forgotten that he didn't have gloves on when he was carrying the box in. Clever but not clever enough.'

'You matched his prints.' It was not a question. If Ferguson knew this much about the man, he had already identified him.

'Yes. He's a small-time crook. His name is Frank Campbell. I've already let Maxwell know so you can start looking for him.'

'Anything else?'

'We found a secret compartment in a chair which Dr Norris used to hide her private papers and other things.'

Gawn decided not to mention she already knew about it.

'Was there anything useful in it?'

'The most interesting thing was a gun case. But no gun.'

She tried to look and sound surprised. 'I didn't know Dr Norris owned a gun.' Which was sort of true. 'And?' She could see the light in his eyes and knew he had found something good. 'What else?'

'Taped under the lining in the gun box was a USB flash drive. Well hidden, obviously not meant to be found.'

She hadn't found it.

'Have you got it?' she asked.

'We've passed it on. We tried to open it but it's encrypted. We couldn't get it opened at all. The computer gurus are working on it now.'

'It must have been important to Dr Norris if she took so much trouble hiding it and it might be what this burglar was looking for and didn't find. Brilliant work, as usual, Mark.' She was happy to be able to congratulate him.

'It's what we do… when we get the chance.'

That was her cue to apologise. She knew she owed him an apology but it wouldn't come easy to her. It was something she hadn't had a lot of practice at. It had been drummed into her by her first commanding officer that it could be seen as a sign of weakness, and as a female officer in predominantly a man's world, she couldn't afford to be seen as weak. She still couldn't.

'OK. You want me to grovel, apologise, is that it? Well, OK, I apologise, Mark. I should have left it to you and your team but we didn't have a search warrant when I was there. We would have had to wait and I needed to see if Jenny Norris was in the apartment, dead or alive.'

'I know she's your friend, ma'am.' Then she saw his body language change. He seemed to relax. 'And I know if I was in trouble, I'd want you on my side bending the rules to help me.'

'Then we're good?'

She stood up, walked round the desk and held out her hand. After a moment's hesitation, he stood up and shook it. Then she noticed a twitch at the corner of his mouth and he couldn't help himself breaking out into a wide smile.

'I had you sweating there for a bit, ma'am, didn't I?'

'You bast…' She didn't finish what she was going to say.

He gave a hearty laugh and then she started laughing too.

'Next time you want to go off on an unsanctioned search, ma'am, let me know.'

'Why? Would you come with me?'

'For one of our own? You bet.'

Chapter 28

Gawn sat at her desk for a few minutes after Ferguson left, doing nothing, just glad to have the meeting over. She thought she had gotten off lightly. He could have reported her to McDowell for what she had done. It was one thing to be regarded as unorthodox but she didn't want to get the reputation for being a renegade who broke the law instead of upholding it. She was glad to get the encounter over so she could get back to concentrating on the case.

She was jotting down some ideas. They were more random thoughts really when a knock came to the door. She wondered who or what was coming next.

'Come.' She crumpled up the top sheet in frustration. None of it made any sense to her.

Maxwell's grinning face appeared around the door. She realised instantly that he had known what Ferguson had planned.

'You knew!' His expression had given him away. She took the scrunched-up page and threw it at him.

'Missed.'

'If I'd wanted to hit you, you'd know all about it.' She smiled back. 'I suppose I deserved it,' she reluctantly conceded.

'He just wanted to make a point, boss. We're a team. Sometimes you seem to forget that. We look out for each other. And Jenny's a member of our team too.'

'I know but I didn't want to put him in a difficult position, or you or any of the others. I knew I was pushing the boundaries and, if it came out, I could be disciplined. It could still be a problem if it comes to a court case and a clever barrister wants to muddy the prosecution. I can afford to lose my job.' She saw the look on his face. 'I have my army pension and money I inherited from my family. To lose my job wouldn't be the disaster for me that it would be for you. You're building your career and you've got a family depending on you. So does Mark. Anyway I could always just sail off into the sunset and join Seb on a beach in California.' It was her attempt to lighten the mood. But even as she said it, she knew just how much she would hate losing her job. It was her life.

Maxwell's expression showed what he thought of that idea.

'I can't quite see you being happy in a bikini on the beach all day and partying with the luvvies all night. You wouldn't stick it for a week.'

She knew he was right.

'Anyhow, I just wanted to let you know that Erin has something for us,' Maxwell said.

'Right. Let's find out what then.'

Chapter 29

'They got back to us with the info on Dr Norris' phone, ma'am,' McKeown announced as soon as Gawn and Maxwell walked into the squad room.

'About time,' Gawn responded.

The younger woman handed her a printout of the calls and text

messages. The first number she spotted was her own.

'Have you gone through these yet, Erin?'

'No. Not yet, ma'am. They just emailed them over and I printed them off.'

Maxwell was standing beside her. She knew he would expect her to let him see the list. He would expect them to discuss it.

'OK. I'll have a look at it first,' she said. 'Then we'll see what needs to be followed up.'

She turned on her heel without further comment and walked out. She knew there would be some messages between Jenny and her when they had been arranging the trip to Dublin and she would prefer that none of the others knew about that just yet. Not even Maxwell. She took the sheets into her office, poured herself a cup of coffee and sat down behind her desk.

She had highlighted in pink several numbers which showed up frequently, some at unusual times of night and some of very short duration. Then she turned to the text messages. As she thought, they had retrieved the messages she and the pathologist had exchanged. There were also several from the victim and one chilling one received by Jenny on Monday night at just after 9.30. It said: 'We've got your forever friend. Bring what she left with you now or she dies. Slowly and painfully.' There was an attachment. Whatever it was, she needed to see it. She made her way back to McKeown's desk.

'I need to see the attachment which came with this text message, Erin.'

The sergeant scanned quickly down the list until she came to the one Gawn had pointed out. Then she double-clicked the mouse. A photograph started to appear, revealing itself painfully slowly section by section. Before half of it could be seen, Gawn knew what it was so that she watched fascinated until the complete photograph had downloaded. She saw a close-up of the matching necklace to the one she had seen in Jenny's jewellery box. It was hanging around a woman's neck, Harriet's neck. What was also clearly visible was a hand holding a knife to her throat and the look of pure terror on Harriet's face.

Chapter 30

'It seems Tilly Mulligan might have been right. Well, partly right. Someone had been watching Jenny but not because of any battered woman she'd helped.'

Gawn's voice revealed her excitement. Now she had something definite, something to follow up, something which suggested someone else had been at the bungalow and that someone else had threatened Harriet. The photograph was clear evidence of that.

'This wasn't sent from Hughes' phone, was it?' Gawn asked.

'It was a burner phone, ma'am. I suppose he could have used it. We can't trace it,' McKeown said.

Maxwell was clutching a printout of the photograph Gawn had just handed to him. He was studying it carefully.

'We need it enhanced to see if we can get any clues from it but we have to assume that it was used to lure Jenny to the bungalow,' Gawn told him.

'But, if they, whoever they are, were following her, why do it that way? There must have been hundreds of occasions when she was by herself, out running along the Lagan or maybe late at night at the hospital when they could simply have grabbed her.'

'I don't know, Paul, and I'm fed up having to say that. Every time we find out something which seems to help it only gives us more questions to find answers for. Was Jenny the real target on Monday night all along? Was Harriet just collateral damage? But if it was this 'something' that Harri had given Jenny to keep for her that is at the bottom of it all, then Harri was up to her neck in this business too.' Then she realised what she had just said and added, 'No pun intended.'

'We'll maybe get answers to your questions when they manage to open the flash drive. It must have been what they were after.'

'If that's so, then why was it still in Jenny's apartment, Paul? Why didn't she take it with her when she went to Harriet's? If she went over there in response to the text, she should have taken it with her. It makes no sense.'

'Unless she thought she could use it to bargain with. Jenny's a clever woman. She might have figured still having it might stop them killing Harriet and her. It might be what's kept her alive,' he suggested.

'If she is still alive,' Gawn interrupted him. It was the first time she had voiced aloud the thought that Jenny might be dead. 'I suppose you're right. If she'd taken it with her, they might have killed her too.'

'Let's go back to the beginning, boss. How did Jenny and Harriet meet? Do you know?'

'I know what Jenny told me.' Gawn had poured herself a cup of coffee and held up an empty cup to Maxwell.

'No, thanks. Kerri has me on a detox regime. Fruit juice only.'

Gawn pulled a sympathetic face. She realised her prefacing her answer with 'what Jenny told me' sounded as if she was now doubting everything that her friend had said. Then she realised that she had to. They needed to check and double-check everything she had previously assumed to be true.

She walked into Maxwell's office and sat down before answering him.

'According to what Jenny told me, they met at a food bank set up in the church across the road from her apartment. Jenny had taken some groceries to donate and Harriet had been running an art class there for disadvantaged children and been dragged in to helping at the food bank too. They struck up a conversation, found they liked the same local Indian restaurant and ended up going there together for a meal. Jenny said they got on really well and when they found they shared a passion for walking in the Mournes, that was it, really. It became a regular thing for them to have dinner together and to go hill walking at weekends.'

'I'll get someone to go to the food bank and ask around. Maybe someone noticed them together or noticed someone hanging about watching them,' Maxwell suggested. 'And how did you meet Harriet then?'

'It was a couple of weeks ago. Jenny and I were having a quick drink after work in the John Hewitt. Harriet came in with some man and she came across and Jenny introduced us.'

'How?'

'What do you mean "how"?'

'I mean did she introduce you as a friend or what?' Maxwell asked.

Gawn thought carefully. She didn't rush to answer. It had been two weeks ago and a lot had happened since then. It had been a casual night out, nothing important really, except it had also been the day when she had got news back from the clinic in Dublin with an appointment for her consultation and that had been lying heavily on her mind that night.

'I can't honestly remember. I'm not much of a witness. Sorry. But it was a very casual meeting. If it had been anything unusual, I would have noticed and I'm pretty sure she'd have explained afterwards that she and Harri were together.'

'Are you?'

Gawn didn't reply. She couldn't really be sure, could she?

'What about the man Harriet was with? Was it Hughes? Did he come over? Did she introduce him?'

'No, definitely not Hughes. I wouldn't have recognised him then of course but I'm sure Jenny would have commented if it had been Hughes. The man stayed at the table where they'd sat down.'

'Did Harriet say who he was?'

'She didn't say his name. At least I don't think so. Only that he was someone she'd met who was interested in buying one of her paintings. A rich American, I think she said.'

'An American?'

'Yes.'

'And what did he look like?'

'I didn't get a particularly good look at him, Paul. The place was packed and he was across the other side of the room from us, and anyway I wasn't paying particular attention to him.'

She realised she sounded like the worst kind of witness, the kind she hated interviewing. Helpful, but no help at all.

'Come on, Gawn. Try to remember,' Maxwell said trying to encourage her.

Gawn closed her eyes and tried to visualise that night in the bar. She remembered the hubbub all around. It was so noisy she'd had trouble hearing what Jenny was saying when she introduced her to Harriet. She hadn't seen the couple walking in so she couldn't be sure how tall the man was. But he had dark hair, she remembered that. A full head of dark hair tied back in a ponytail. And tanned skin with a slight Mexican or South American look, she thought, but that might only have been because Harriet had said he was American. She told Maxwell.

'Great. That gives us something to work with. An American with a tan and long dark hair.'

'Who might have absolutely nothing to do with any of this. He's probably safely back in New York or Chicago or somewhere with one of Harriet's paintings hanging on his wall.'

'And what about Monday night? What did she say when she phoned you? What time was it?'

'A bit after nine. I'd just changed and was ready for an early night when she rang.'

'That would probably have been just before she got that text message with the picture. How did she sound?'

'We've been over all this.'

They had discussed it briefly on Tuesday morning but now he wanted all the details again. He was right of course, it was important.

'She sounded upset. We'd been talking about Harri and her husband earlier and…'

'You spoke to Jenny during the day on Monday?'

She hadn't told him that before. He wondered what else she might be keeping from him.

'Yes. We had a girly day out in Dublin together.'

She saw the look of surprise on his face. He looked stunned. She wasn't going to start explaining what their trip had really been about. It couldn't have anything to do with the case. She was sure of that. If she could be sure of anything.

But where Jenny had spent the day on Monday was part of their investigation. Time had been wasted trying to trace her movements and she had said nothing about it.

She knew he would be wondering what she was playing at; what she was hiding. Before he could find the words to ask, she continued.

'On the train she told me that she was the one who had convinced Harri to leave her husband.'

'Does he know that?'

'I don't know. Harri might have told him, I suppose.'

'So then when she phoned you?'

'She was upset.'

'Angry?'

'No. I wouldn't say that exactly. Annoyed maybe, but more disappointed than anything.'

'About what?'

'That Harri didn't want to speak to her. Wouldn't discuss anything with her. She had tried talking and Harri had more or less blown her off. She suspected that she was planning to go back to her husband. But I suppose it isn't surprising she didn't want to talk about it if Hughes was there with her at the time as he might have been.'

'So Jenny asked you to speak to Harri instead.'

'Yes. She thought it might sound more objective coming from a police officer. She asked me to explain about cases I knew where women had been killed after going back to their abusive husbands.'

'And you agreed to go and see her?'

Gawn realised herself it sounded a bit out of character for her. The truth was she had felt she owed Jenny a debt. Jenny had helped her get through Monday. She knew her secrets and she had been there when she needed support. She really felt she couldn't refuse even though it wasn't her usual kind of thing at all.

Gawn felt guilty about keeping Maxwell in the dark. She hadn't kept anything important from him. At least she didn't think so.

'Paul, I'm asking you to trust me on this one. I've told you everything that might affect the case.'

She met his eye. Would he believe her? Any further conversation was interrupted by the phone.

'Girvin.'

Maxwell watched her and saw she was getting some news.

'Right. Thank you. Get back to them and let me know as soon as you have anything more.'

She put the receiver down slowly.

'That was Billy. I had him tracing some of the interesting phone numbers on Jenny's call log.'

'And did he get something?'

'Yes. The phone making the late-night calls is a burner.'

'Nothing surprising there then. So we can't trace who it belongs to.' Maxwell's voice was flat.

'But it's turned on at the minute so we can find out where it is.'

'What are we waiting for?'

'They're working on getting us an exact location or as close as they can but I don't want to just charge in, Paul. We don't know what we're facing. We could walk into the middle of God knows what. Who they are, what they want, how Jenny ties in to it and what, if anything, the flash drive has to do with it, we just don't know. If Jenny is still alive and we charge in, they could kill her. We need to set up surveillance first.'

'Let's do that then. As soon as we get a location, I'll put a team on it.'

She was glad he rushed off then to start organising a surveillance team. It stopped him questioning her any more about Monday and why she hadn't said anything earlier about being with Jenny. But she knew he wouldn't just forget about it. At some point, she'd have to tell him.

Chapter 31

'They're all in place, ma'am. The first shift started just after midnight.'

Maxwell had arranged round-the-clock surveillance of one of the narrow little streets of terraced houses off Cregagh Road in East Belfast. They had managed to get access to a vacant property halfway down the street from a friendly local estate agent, where the team would be based, and they had two cars, one parked on the main road and one at the end of the street watching comings and goings ready to follow anyone of interest. Their only problem was, they didn't know exactly who that might be.

'We're really working in the dark here. Do we have any idea who we're looking for?' he asked.

'Not really, Paul. The phone's somewhere there. But they couldn't identify an individual house for us.'

She couldn't keep a whole team watching a street without a specific target for very long. It was too heavy on manpower with no guarantees it would turn up anything to help them. They couldn't follow every man who came in or out of the street. They needed something to narrow it down. She had hoped that follow-up inquiries at the mortuary and Jenny's apartment might have turned up a description of someone following her as Tilly had suggested, but no one had noticed anyone following or watching Jenny.

She heard the squad room door opening behind her and was surprised to see Robert Boyd walking in. He was an imposing figure of a man. Coming up towards retirement, he was universally respected among his colleagues. His 6'3" frame was reassuringly solid, the kind of copper you'd like beside you in a tight spot, and, although his salt-and-pepper hair was thinning slightly now, he looked fit and younger than his years.

'Chief Inspector, could I have a word with you in private?'

His voice was unexpectedly serious. She wondered what he could have to say to her that had necessitated a trip to her office to speak to her in person.

Gawn was surprised. Boyd had said he would keep an ear out for anything to help but she had thought it unlikely she would hear from him again. So why was he here?

'Come into my office, Robert.'

He followed her and she indicated an armchair.

'Would you like some coffee or I could rustle up some tea if you prefer that?'

'No. No thanks. This is just a quick visit.'

She sat down on the other armchair and waited for him to speak.

'You have men watching a house in Ardenvohr Street.'

This was not a question. He obviously knew she did.

'Yes. How did you know?'

'Because I have an ongoing surveillance operation there.'

She was surprised and then immediately delighted. If Boyd already suspected something criminal was going on there, it would almost certainly be at the same location. The possibility of two different criminals living and working out of the same street was low. Not impossible of course, but unlikely.

She had already been surprised when word had come through that their target phone was located somewhere in Ardenvohr Street. She knew the area, knew the street. It was a quiet, respectable residential area and it was only round the corner from where her father had once been stationed when she was a child. She remembered visits to the now demolished Willowfield Police Barracks. She had loved to go there as any visit included a trip to the local

Italian ice cream parlour. She wondered if it was still there. She pulled her mind back to the present.

'There is something dodgy going on there then?'

'One of the gangs who've been running girls is Romanian. Their leader is Danut Vacarescu – it's pronounced dahnoots but it's spelt D-a-n-u-t and my men think it's a very appropriate name. He has a bit of a reputation for being crazy. They just refer to him as Nuts, I'm afraid. He keeps a woman and child in Ardenvohr Street. He has an apartment down near Bridge End himself but he visits the woman and we think he uses it for meetings and passing things on. We've been watching the house for several weeks, logging the comings and goings; trying to identify as many of his men as possible before we move on them.'

'And now my men have turned up in the middle of it all.'

'Yes. One of my team recognized one of yours sitting in a car along the street and that set the alarm bells ringing. I'm only glad you didn't go rushing in and scare them all off.'

'We've got a phone linked to our case making calls from somewhere in this street. We just can't pinpoint exactly where. If we'd had a specific target, I suppose we might have rushed in,' she had to admit.

'Thank God for that then. Weeks of work would have gone down the toilet if you had.'

'Sorry, Robert.'

She wasn't sure exactly what she was apologising for. They hadn't known about his surveillance and, if they had, she would have spoken to him first, not gone rushing in.

'I suppose you want us to hang back.'

'I want you to clear out,' said Boyd. 'These guys aren't exactly geniuses but lots of new men appearing in the street and strange cars sitting parked day and night, I think even they might notice. I'll give you anything we have and pass on anything else we get but I want your men out of there today. As soon as possible.'

She tapped her index finger off her lip as if she was thinking over what he was asking. She knew she was going to agree. She didn't really have a choice. If Boyd took it upstairs she would be ordered to stand them down. She knew that. She just wanted to keep him waiting a minute or two to emphasise how important this was for her investigation so he would be sure to do what he said and so he would owe her. It was always useful to have a few people who owed you a favour.

'Of course. I'll get them out of there straightaway. Sorry, Robert.'

She saw him relax into the chair and realised he had expected an argument, maybe even a refusal. Her reputation as a renegade who did her own thing and ignored orders must really have grown.

'So what can you tell me now?'

'Nuts is not the top man but he's a trusted second in command and a heavy. He has a part-time job at a gym at Dundonald and his muscles show it. I wouldn't want to take him on mano a mano. He visits the house regularly to see his girlfriend and stops over several nights a week, but he also meets up with some of the rest of the gang there and we've seen the odd young girl passing through too.'

'And done nothing about it?'

'I explained this to you already, Gawn. We rush in and save one wee girl, arrest one man and they shut down there and move on somewhere else. We watch, we follow and eventually we get a whole bunch of villains and put them behind bars or send them back to their own country and, if we're lucky, we rescue a lot of women. That's how it works.'

'I understand.'

She could see from his eyes that he wasn't comfortable with having to abandon any woman but he knew his job and he was good at it.

'Anything you've got so far that could help my case?'

'Well, Jenny Norris has never been there. I can tell you that much. But we did follow one of the men from the house to Newcastle a couple of weekends ago. He didn't seem to do anything when he was there and it was just logged and forgotten about, but I was rereading the report and I noticed that at one point my man thought his target seemed to be following a Land Rover. It could have been a coincidence but I know Dr Norris drives a Land Rover, doesn't she?'

Gawn nodded.

'Your man didn't see Jenny or my victim?'

'It wasn't in the report so I questioned him this morning before I came over here. He doesn't know Jenny Norris. He's never had occasion to attend a PM so he wouldn't have recognised her even if he had seen her and he wouldn't have known your victim either. He says there were a lot of people in Donard Park that day, but he didn't recognise anyone of interest to our case. I'll have him go through all the photographs he took to see if he can spot Norris or your victim in them. If he does, I'll let you know.'

He stood up as he spoke signalling an end to their conversation.

'Thank you, Robert. Could we get copies of all his photographs and I'll have my people go through them? That would probably be quicker and easier. They know who they're looking for.'

'Of course. Good luck, Gawn.'

Two steps forward, one step back. The old saying came into her thoughts as she watched Boyd's back retreating down the corridor. They seemed to make some progress and then they found more difficulties and barriers and now more suspects too.

Chapter 32

McKeown, Grant and Dee had spread photographs over the table in an empty conference room along the corridor from the Serious Crimes suite. Now they were trawling carefully through them. Dee had a magnifying glass and was searching the faces of people in the background of the pictures.

Gawn opened the door and walked in.

'Any progress?' she asked.

'We think we've spotted Dr Norris' car.'

McKeown handed Gawn a picture so she could see for herself.

'Have you been looking through all these photographs? Take a break and I'll see if I can get digital copies for you.'

'Thanks, boss.'

The three detectives made their way out of the room heading to the canteen, glad to get a break. Gawn stared thoughtfully at the picture in her hand. She was still in that pose when Maxwell opened the door and walked in.

'We've pulled the team out of Ardenvohr Street,' he informed her.

'Good. Can you get on to someone in the PPU, Paul, and ask them to send their surveillance photographs digitally? Boyd's already okayed it for us to look at them. We really don't need to destroy another rainforest to do it.'

'Will do. And they've found our burglar, Frank Campbell.'

'Great. Now for some answers. Are they bringing him here?'

'No. They found him on waste ground near the docks. Just about alive. He's in the ICU at the Royal. They don't know whether he'll make it. Whoever these people are, they don't like leaving loose ends. And Jenny's definitely one of those.'

The look they exchanged said what she couldn't put into words.

* * *

An hour later when Gawn was making her way through the squad room to speak to Maxwell, she found McKeown, Grant and Dee all busy at their computers.

'Thanks, boss. We got all the surveillance pictures. We've made a start on them but there's a lot, hundreds. They've been watching the house for weeks.'

'They sent everything over?'

'Seems like it. Yeah.'

Gawn was about to tell her sergeant to ignore everything except the ones from Newcastle when something made her stop. If they had the photographs, they might as well check through them all. They might get lucky and be able to recognise someone else associated with their case. If they could identify some of the other men, she could take the pictures to Tilly and see if she'd seen any of them before, and they could question the staff at the mortuary and at Jenny's apartment in case anyone had been hanging around watching her. It was a long shot but they didn't have much else at the minute.

Chapter 33

'Here you are, ma'am.' McKeown handed a folder to Gawn as she walked past. 'It was a heck of a lot quicker and easier working on the photos on the computer.'

'And what did you find, Erin? Anything useful?'

'There weren't any of Dr Norris in Newcastle. If the suspect followed her on foot from the car park, the tail missed it. These are all men who made regular or at least multiple visits to the house in Ardenvohr Street over the past month or so. But there's one here I think you'll be especially interested in. He only appeared once. I put it on top.'

Gawn opened the folder and she couldn't help reacting when she saw the picture. Edward Hughes.

'Hughes was at the house?'

'Only once. At least, only once they got a photograph of him. It was taken on Monday afternoon at about three o'clock.'

'The same day his wife was murdered?'

'Yes, ma'am.'

'What has a respectable scientist cum businessman got to do with a criminal gang from Eastern Europe? Good work, Erin. Good work, guys,' she said raising her voice to make sure Grant and Dee could hear too, then walked into Maxwell's office.

He was seated at his desk. He had loosened his tie and undone the top button of his shirt. It looked like he was expecting to be there for a while.

'You've seen these?' She held out the folder.

'Not yet but Erin told me what they'd found. What do we do now? Question Hughes? We could pull him in. We have him associating with known criminals.'

'No. We can't do that. If we question him about associating with the Romanians, you can be sure word will get back to them, probably through Hartnett. They'll disappear into the night like snow off a ditch and start all over again somewhere else. Boyd's case will be up in smoke and my name'll be mud for wasting all their hard work. Anyway Hughes could claim he called at the wrong house and that he doesn't know anything about the people who live there. We need more to tie him to them.'

'We can't just ignore it.'

'Of course we can't ignore it. But we'll need to tread carefully. It puts Hughes in a very different light, doesn't it? And who's this woman in the photograph with him? Could that be Hughes' lady friend? I'll need to speak to Boyd.'

She looked at her watch.

'It's probably too late now. I'll set up a meeting with him, speak to him first thing tomorrow morning. Go home, Paul and spend some time with your family. I've a feeling we'll be pulling a lot more overtime over the next couple of days. Whoever has Jenny, if she's still alive' – her voice quivered as she spoke the words – 'they'll need to get rid of her soon. She's a liability unless they think she still has something they want, like the flash drive. She doesn't have it of course but maybe they think she does. That might be enough to keep her alive for now, but her time is limited and God knows what they're putting her through to try to get her to talk. The clock is ticking for us to find her before they decide to give up and cut their losses.'

Chapter 34

Robert Boyd appeared in Gawn's office very soon after she arrived there on Saturday morning even though she was early. He knocked but didn't wait for a reply before walking in. He didn't look to be in a good mood. In fact, he looked ready for an argument.

'What's this about identifying your suspect at my Romanian's house?'

No time for 'Good mornings' today. He towered over her at her desk and she noticed how his brows were knitted together in annoyance, almost forming a straight line over his already hooded blue eyes.

'Our victim's husband was at the house in Ardenvohr Street on the day of the murder.'

She stated the fact baldly, not trying to justify or explain anything. Boyd was a good detective. She didn't need to point out the importance of this discovery or its implications. He realised immediately what it meant. He sat down opposite her, some of the spirit gone out of him.

'And I suppose you're going to pull him in and question him about it now?'

'No. Not immediately. I was waiting to speak to you, Robert, otherwise I would have had him picked up last night.'

His expression changed. He relaxed.

'How did you even get hold of our surveillance pictures anyway?'

'My inspector asked for the photographs to be sent over digitally and someone at your end sent over everything you had. You couldn't have expected my team not to look at them all.'

Whoever had sent them, had done them a big favour. They might never have connected Hughes with the gang otherwise or at least not until it was too late.

'I see. I wasn't keeping the other photographs from you deliberately, Gawn. I just didn't think they had anything to do with your case.'

'Let's call it serendipity then and see where we go from here,' she suggested, smiling at him. 'Coffee?' She moved across to pour herself a cup.

'Too early for me. Thanks anyway. And thank you for not charging in and buggering up my whole case.'

'I don't want to do that but I can't afford to sit on my hands waiting too long before acting. There's a woman's life at stake.'

'Jenny Norris. Yes, of course.' Boyd nodded his understanding.

‘Do you think your Romanians could be involved in my murder case? Does it sound like something they would do?’

‘What? Kill someone? In a heartbeat some of them, but only if there was something in it for them. Who is this Hughes? What does he do? Is he wealthy? Could he afford to pay to have his wife killed?’

‘You tell me. What’s the going rate for a wife’s murder these days?’

‘I wouldn’t know.’

‘Tell me, Robert, who’s this woman with Hughes? Is it Nuts’ girlfriend?’

She held out the photograph to him.

‘No. That’s not Miriam, the girlfriend. This woman was never at the house before. It’s not a very good image of her, side-faced like that and her hair over most of her face. We haven’t got around to trying to identify her yet. She wasn’t a high priority for us.’

‘Well, I think she might be for me. I’m going to try to find out who she is and how she’s connected to Hughes. If we trace her, I won’t make a move against her until I’ve spoken to you but I can’t afford to wait around, Robert. How quickly do you think you can move against these people?’

‘Ideally we’d have taken another week or at least a couple of days but I realise we don’t have that kind of timescale now. We’ll move it all up and make our move tonight. Once we have them in custody, you’re welcome to question Nuts or anyone else we pick up. If we get Hughes and the mystery woman, I’ll let you know.’

‘Thank you, Robert. I hope it all goes well for you tonight.’

Chapter 35

'Paul, do we still have a tail on Hughes?'

Gawn had made her way to Maxwell's office as soon as Boyd had left.

'No. I pulled them off after we spoke to him at the factory.'

'Damn. I should have told you to keep him under surveillance. We need to find out where he is. Now. Nobody approaches him but we need to have him in view at all times. If he did pay the Romanians to kill his wife, then he knows something about Jenny's abduction and that makes him valuable to us but dangerous to them. They may contact him or even try to shut him up like Frank Campbell. And we need to find out who this woman is.'

She thrust the photograph of Hughes and the mystery woman towards Maxwell and let it drop down onto his desk in front of him.

'You think she has something to do with the murder?'

'I don't know. Maybe they just happened to arrive at the front door at the same time. But there's something vaguely familiar about her.'

'You think you've seen her somewhere before?'

'I don't know.' She was racking her brain and she was annoyed with herself that she wasn't finding any answers. 'Maybe Janine.'

'Who the hell's Janine, Gawn? Is this something else you've been holding back from me?'

She was shocked. She knew how uptight and worried she felt about Jenny's disappearance, but she hadn't given much thought to how it was affecting Maxwell.

'Janine was one of the women I saw at the house in Newcastle. But it's not her. I'm sure. There's just something familiar about the line of this woman's jaw or something. I wish we had a better picture. This probably won't be much good for facial rec.'

He was already on the phone giving instructions for an immediate search for Hughes.

'It might be worthwhile making another trip to Altor, Paul. We could have a word with Hughes' boss and find out exactly what he's been working on. It must be something that would interest these Romanians. There has to be a connection. Altor creates tests which must involve drugs. But Boyd said the Romanians weren't into pushing drugs.'

'Do you really think there'll be anyone there on a Saturday?' Maxwell asked.

'Maybe or maybe not but I just need to get out of the office. I can't just sit here doing nothing. It's going to be a long day waiting for Boyd's raid tonight. Let's try and see.'

'I'll get the word out to find Hughes.'

'But not to stop him. We don't want to tip him off.'

'Yes, boss. Understood.'

Chapter 36

Altor Pharmaceuticals looked almost the same. Perhaps even slightly less impressive and even less busy than their last visit. There was only a handful of cars in the small car park along with a large van with its back doors standing open. While they watched, two men in brown overalls carried a heavy box out and put it inside the van.

'Well, someone's working today anyway,' Maxwell said.

Gawn placed her hand on Maxwell's arm. He felt her grip tighten slightly.

'That box.' Gawn sounded excited.

'Yes?'

'The palm tree logo on it.'

'Yes?' Maxwell could see the logo but he didn't understand why it was important.

'I've seen it before.'

'Where?' Maxwell asked.

'In Jenny's apartment. Campbell had carried it in as cover if anyone asked what he was doing there. He was posing as a delivery man, remember? I never thought the box itself had any significance.'

The two men had gone into the building leaving the back doors of the van lying open. Maxwell glanced inside as he walked past. He read the company name on the box.

'It's the logo for Eureka Advances. They're the partner company for Altor, aren't they? Why wouldn't they be sending something to them?' Maxwell asked.

'Right. Altor's partner company. OK.' She was trying to clarify her thinking. 'But it's a freaky coincidence that Frank Campbell just happened to have a Eureka box to hand when he broke into Jenny's apartment. Eureka is involved in this somehow and that means Altor is too. I don't know how yet but I'm sure they are. We can follow it up later. We don't want to tip anyone off and put Jenny's life in any more danger.'

Gawn's mood had improved. Maybe all the different strands of the investigation were beginning to come together. She couldn't make sense of them yet or how they were linked, but it was progress – of a kind. It had made their journey here worthwhile even if they didn't get to question anybody.

The doorbell brought the same response from the same receptionist. They recognised her voice. When she buzzed them in and they walked across to face her behind her desk she looked up and smiled in a disinterested sort of way.

'I'm afraid Dr Hughes isn't here today. He's left the company.'

Gawn and Maxwell exchanged looks. Hughes must have cleared out almost immediately after they'd spoken to him.

'It's not Dr Hughes we're here to see. We'd like to speak to whoever's in charge, your manager or CEO.'

As she spoke Gawn realised they should at least have checked the name of whoever was in charge. Coming here had been an impulse act. It could have been a wasted journey but for spotting the box.

'Is Mr Rodway expecting you?'

'No. He's not. But tell him we won't keep him long and it's very important.'

The receptionist didn't invite them to sit and Gawn wouldn't have complied anyway. The young woman lifted the phone. Gawn tapped her fingers on the reception desk as she listened and waited.

'Mr Rodway, there are two police officers here. They'd like to speak to you.' There was a pause while she listened to the voice on the other end of the phone. 'About Dr Hughes.'

Gawn watched the young woman's face.

'Yes, sir. I'll bring them along now.' She stood up and turned to them. 'Follow me.'

Once through a set of heavy doors they found themselves in a short bright corridor painted in a restful pale blue with concealed lighting along the edges of the ceiling. There were original paintings of local scenes adorning the walls. This was obviously the executive side of the business where clients were brought to be impressed. Gawn was surprised to spot the initials HH on a painting of Carrickfergus Castle.

The receptionist knocked on the door and when an American voice came from within, she opened it and stood back to let them walk through, then moved away, her job done. This office was grander but presented a less modern vibe than Hughes'. No doubt deliberately so, Gawn thought to herself. The furniture was heavy dark wood, solid, suggesting stability and success. It looked posed as did the man behind the desk who stood up to greet them.

Gawn would not have been surprised if he had greeted them with a 'Howdy'. He walked around from behind his desk and extended his hand to Maxwell. When he spoke, he did indeed have a faint Southern drawl but mixed with a Belfast accent.

'Chief Inspector. How can I help?'

'Mr Rodway, I'm *Inspector* Maxwell.'

'*I'm* Chief Inspector Girvin.'

Gawn didn't mind Rodwell's mistake. It had been made before. But it had flustered him a little.

'My apologies, Chief Inspector. A silly assumption on my part. A lot of my most senior scientists and associates are females these days.'

He was trying to backtrack but instead was digging himself into a deeper hole.

'It's quite alright, sir. Forget it.' She wanted to make him believe she was reasonable and a bit of a pushover. 'We'd appreciate your help, sir.'

'Of course. How can I help you?'

He smiled at her trying to exude some charm and signalled she should take a seat. She ignored the offer.

'You know we were here before, talking to Dr Hughes,' she said.

'Yes, of course. Absolutely awful what happened to poor Harriet.'

'Did you know Mrs Hughes?'

'Yes. Of course. She was a talented artist. You may have noticed a couple of her paintings in the corridor on your way in. And she was one of our investors, of course.'

'Harriet Hughes invested in this company?'

She was surprised by this news. They weren't looking into Harriet's finances too closely, only her husband's. It hadn't seemed important before. It did now. They would have to. Another job for Walter Pepper. It might have been more than mortgage papers Hughes was trying to get his wife to sign. And more of an issue for him if she wouldn't. Enough to get her killed?

'Mrs Hughes put money into the company when we took it over and decided to stay in Northern Ireland rather than moving everything elsewhere.'

'When was this?'

'Two years ago.'

'So, after her husband was already working for Altor?'

'Yes. Edward had been working for the original owners but when we took over we had a choice of developing this site or moving operations to the Philippines and at that point Harriet offered to invest.'

Gawn realised Rodway wasn't talking about a few pounds. A sizable sum of money must have been invested to ensure the factory remained here and Edward kept his job. Where had Harriet got money like that? She was an art teacher and any teacher she had ever met complained about what they were paid.

'I believe Dr Hughes has left your employment now.'

'Yes. Not wholly unexpected, I'm afraid. Edward has always been ambitious. His work was always… satisfactory.' His voice lingered over the word 'satisfactory', inviting the detectives to take out of it what they would. 'But I can say now that if it hadn't been for his wife's investment, we'd probably have got rid of him some time ago. We were prepared to let him develop some of his own little projects in his own time. We knew eventually he would want to branch out on his own and that suited us fine.'

'It didn't worry you that he was working on something else? I thought industrial espionage was a major thing for big companies?' Maxwell chipped in.

'Edward's research wasn't related to anything we were working on here. And I doubt very much if anything he developed would go anywhere. I was confident there was no conflict of interest.'

He smiled trying to convince them. Gawn watched his eyes. His mouth was smiling but his eyes were giving nothing away.

'And what was he working on exactly?' Gawn asked. She felt they had missed an opportunity to question Hughes himself about this.

'He never told me in detail but I know he'd developed an interest in Huntington's disease. I think he was working on a screening test.'

'Wouldn't that be a big moneymaker, sir, something your company might like to own the rights to?' Maxwell asked.

'Depends what you compare it to, officer. It might be an advance but there already are tests to indicate if parents carry the gene.'

'So not every child gets it?' Gawn asked.

'No. And having a test mightn't prove as popular as you might suppose and the expense involved in the development of the test could be prohibitive. It wouldn't be like finding a cure for cancer which is what my company is working on.' He spoke, pride sounding in his voice. 'So, to go back to your original question, we weren't concerned about Edward's off-the-books work. It wasn't going to affect us.'

Gawn wondered exactly what other off-the-books work might go on here.

'I see.' Gawn was thinking furiously. She wanted to know why Hughes had an interest in Huntington's disease. Did he have some personal reason?

'Do you know why Dr Hughes was interested in Huntington's?'

'I'm afraid not, Chief Inspector.'

'Or where he's gone?'

'No. He didn't share that information with me. His leaving was rather… sudden. I expected he would go but not so soon or so quickly. He did what I think is usually referred to as a "moonlight flit". One day he was here, the next he and all his belongings were gone. I assumed he'd had a good offer to take his research to some of the companies already working on Huntington's.'

'Thank you, sir. You've been very helpful. One last thing. Would it be possible for us to take a quick look around Dr Hughes' office?' Gawn asked.

'I'm afraid it wouldn't do you very much good. Edward cleared it out completely. And his replacement has already moved in. There's nothing of Edward's left there now.'

Neither Hughes nor Rodway had wasted much time. Hughes must have left almost immediately after they had spoken to him and Rodway had found a replacement very quickly, if she was to believe him. So, a dead end. Nothing more to be learned here. At least for now, Gawn thought.

But Rodway seemed too reasonable to her. What sort of boss doesn't care that an employee is working using their equipment and premises to develop something which could be worth millions and they would get no benefit from? She wasn't sure she believed anything he had told them.

Rodway had appeared keen to help but the whole time they were speaking he had never met her eyes directly, always talking into the void between the two police officers as if afraid he might give something away and she had noted a nervousness in his voice which made her think he was hiding something. But was it anything to do with Jenny Norris?

Chapter 37

'Interesting.'

'Very. I'm glad we came. I wonder why the company CEO was working on a Saturday? Could it have something to do with the boxes being shipped out? Something's going on here, Paul, but it might have nothing to do with Jenny's disappearance or Harriet's murder.'

'They have links with that Eureka place. It's not surprising they send stuff to them. It would be more surprising if they didn't,' Maxwell argued. 'Working on a Saturday is just the American way. They work long hours.'

Gawn ignored what he had said.

'I'm afraid I've been guilty of underestimating our victim. I'd assumed Harriet Hughes was just your typical teacher, typical downtrodden wife, typical everything. Now it seems there was a lot more to her. She obviously had quite a bit of money and we need to find out where she got it and who gets it now. If Hughes is the beneficiary – which is most likely – then that would be another motive for him to kill her, wouldn't it? If he needed money for this new company he's setting up, he might have thought that was an easy way to get it. And, if there's money behind it all, he might have paid someone to kill her for him.'

'Walter's already started on their finances but I'll get him to prioritise Harriet's bank accounts and he can check about her will as well. He likes the financial stuff.'

'He'll not be able to do much before Monday. Let's hope we can trace her husband in the meantime. Talk about attracting attention to yourself. If we hadn't been suspicious of him before, he runs off immediately after we've spoken to him. He's certainly no criminal mastermind,' Gawn said.

'You don't need to be to bash someone to death with a rock.'

* * *

Maxwell insisted they stop at a drive-through on their way back. He had missed lunch and he knew they had a long night ahead of them with Boyd's raid going ahead. He knew Gawn would want to wait, all night if necessary, to see what happened and interview Nuts if they got him. So he introduced her to the delights of an all-day breakfast wrap from a Canadian franchise which had recently opened in Belfast.

'Don't be telling Kerri about me eating this. She'd go crazy.'

'Promise.' Gawn smiled conspiratorially and took her first bite. She looked pleasantly surprised. It tasted good. 'This isn't bad.'

'Nothing but gourmet dining for me, boss. You know that.'

He smiled back. This was a bit like it had been between them when he had been her rookie sergeant. They had been good days.

* * *

As soon as they'd finished they headed back. The team was working flat out including a number of probationary constables who Gawn had 'borrowed' for work experience, as she'd told their training officer. They were trying to identify Jenny Norris' route from the bungalow to the sailing club. They had sourced a lot of CCTV footage. They needed to know if she had driven there herself or been driven or if she'd even been in the vehicle or been dumped somewhere en route.

'Anything, Erin?'

'We've managed to get an ANPR ping on the Land Rover on the Upper Newtownards Road at Knock junction.'

'What time?'

'Just after midnight, ma'am.'

'Was Dr Norris driving?'

'No. It was a man.'

'Was Dr Norris in the vehicle?'

'Not in the front seat. We couldn't really see into the back.'

'Sergeant!' The call came from two young trainees sharing a computer screen.

'Sorry, ma'am,' McKeown said.

'That's OK. What is it?' Gawn turned her attention to a fresh-faced trainee, who looked nervously at her.

'We noticed that when we started tracing the Land Rover's route back from Knock, nearly every time we saw it the same car was behind them or within a car or two of them.'

'What make of car?'

'A dark blue BMW, ma'am,' his female counterpart spoke up more confidently.

'Did you get the number plate?'

'We got a partial.'

'Erin, get the images over to Tech and see if they can do anything with them. Try running it, even the partial. They dumped the Land Rover but they might still have the BMW. Find it and we might find them.' Gawn turned to the two young recruits. 'What are your names?'

'Declan Murphy, ma'am.'

'Anna Magill.'

'Declan and Anna, well done,' Gawn said. 'I'll be letting your training officer know how pleased I am with your work.'

She turned back to McKeown.

'Have you had a break, Erin?'

She was aware she and Maxwell had had a change of scenery and then had taken that short time for something to eat. She didn't want to push the others too hard. They would need to be at their most alert going through the rest of the footage or they could easily miss something vital.

'We got some sandwiches.'

'Well, after you've sent the images off, take a few minutes and have a coffee or something.'

'Thanks, ma'am.'

Gawn proceeded into Maxwell's office. He was already behind his desk, jacket off, tie off too this time. He was just in the act of rolling up the shirt sleeves. He looked like he was preparing for a long night.

'You look ready for action. If only we can trace the BMW now.' She explained what Erin's team had found.

'I've told Walter to dig into Harriet's finances. He's already started on Hughes' but he hasn't had much luck. The man doesn't seem to have much in the way of assets. A few thousand in his bank account and half of the house which is mortgaged. He hasn't traced anything to do with him setting up a new company. Not in Northern Ireland anyway. He's making a start now on some of Harriet's personal papers they managed to salvage from the bungalow to see if they turn up anything interesting. He'll get on to her bank first thing on Monday morning and he's trying to find her solicitor to see about a will. It'll hardly be Hartnett.' He laughed mirthlessly. 'And I've just checked the reports about Hughes. No sightings. And some bad news I'm afraid.'

She didn't ask what. She knew he would tell her whatever it was.

'Campbell didn't make it.'

Gawn turned her back to him and stood looking out over the squad room. These people had killed Campbell, just a small-time career criminal who had failed them and who could identify them, so what chance did Jenny have if they had taken her? She swung back suddenly.

'Give me fifteen minutes, Paul, and then come to my office.'

Chapter 38

It was Saturday evening, the time when she and Seb facetimed each week. But she couldn't. Not tonight. Much as she would have loved to forget all about the case and talk to him about silly things; to tease him about how many film stars he had spotted out and about in the coffee shops and restaurants of Santa Monica which he now frequented; she couldn't. Not tonight. Jenny's life was hanging in the balance. At least, she hoped it was. She didn't want to consider the alternative. That she was already dead and a few hours one way or the other wouldn't make any difference.

Gawn removed her jacket and hung it carefully over the back of her chair. She sat down. Secrets. Her secrets. Keeping secrets. Everyone had them but sometimes they could lead to murder. What secrets had Harriet Hughes had? Gawn undid her necklace and removed her wedding ring from the chain. Then she placed it on her finger. She dialled Seb's number. He answered and she couldn't help smiling at the sound of his voice.

'Hi, babe. You're late. I was beginning to think you'd forgotten or maybe you had a hot date. Hey, why aren't we facetiming? You've not got a man there with you, have you?'

'Of course not. I'm still in the office. No man. Unless you count Paul.'

'He doesn't count. Kerri would kill him if he stepped out of line.' He laughed. 'You're in the office on a Saturday night? It must be a big case.'

'It is. People trafficking. I'm just waiting for word about a raid to take the gang down.'

'You're not there with them?'

He knew how much she liked to be in the middle of the action, not sitting back waiting for news.

'No. I'm here at my desk but I can't facetime. McDowell could sweep in without warning.'

'OK. I believe you.'

He sounded disappointed and she realised he enjoyed their weekly calls and seeing her every bit as much as she did. With all his excitement, all the wonderful things he was able to do in California, how his boyhood dreams were being realised, he missed her. She didn't think she deserved to be loved the way Sebastian loved her but she was just so grateful he did. He had saved her so many times, in so many ways. And having him in her life had made her a better person.

Reluctantly she said, 'I'm gonna have to go, darling. It could all kick off at any minute. I just wanted to hear your voice. I miss you.'

'I miss you more,' he responded.

'No, seriously.'

'I am being serious, Gawn. I miss you. I don't know what I would do if I lost you.'

'Well, you're not going to lose me.'

'Be careful.'

'I will. I promise. I love you.'

'Love you more, babe.'

And she ended the call. She wondered what her team would think if they could have heard that conversation. The Ice Queen, the tough no-nonsense boss who often had grown men quivering in their boots when they crossed her, the bitch. Those names and more, she knew. She hadn't minded the names before and now she thought it was a useful shield to hide behind. She couldn't afford to be seen as a bleeding heart. She had to be careful not to get too soft. Not if she wanted to do her job well.

Maxwell knocked and walked in.

'Ready?' he asked.

'Yes.' She pushed her hair back off her face. He noticed the ring on her finger.

Before either had time to say anything more, Gawn's phone rang.

'Girvin.'

Maxwell could see a flash of excitement in her eyes.

'Robert. How'd it go? Wait a minute. I'll put you on speakerphone. I have Maxwell here with me.'

Robert Boyd's voice boomed out of the speaker. He sounded elated.

'We got them. All of them. The whole bloomin' lot. It went like a dream. You did us a favour, Gawn. We would have waited another week to try to make sure everything was perfect. We didn't know they were planning a major move of their assets tonight. We caught them red-handed.'

'Assets?' Maxwell queried.

'A group of women picked up from the ferry to be taken down south. If we'd left it until tomorrow they would have been spread out all over the country. Instead we were able to intercept them where they had the women packed in a van like sardines on the A1 just outside Banbridge. And we got the others in different houses with smuggled cigarettes, and alcohol and some drugs. Even a small number of handguns. We haven't traced where they came from yet but some of them will talk and we might be able to link them to attacks or murders.'

'And what about Nuts and his girlfriend and the house in Ardenvohr Street?' Gawn asked.

'Yes, we got him and Miriam. He was in the van with the girls so he's no chance of getting out of this one. My team's turning over the house in Ardenvohr Street and his apartment as we speak. He was armed so we have him for the weapon too. But that's all just for starters.'

'And when can I get to question him?'

'I thought you might like to start by speaking to his girlfriend.'

Boyd had hesitated before making the suggestion. He wanted to have first go at Nuts himself. He'd invested a lot of time and effort into this case and he felt he deserved to get first crack at questioning the main man. He was the one who could connect them to the really big bosses, if they could get him to talk. He didn't want anyone else interfering in that process.

'You're not trying to fob me off with some woman who knows nothing about anything, are you?'

'No. I said I didn't think she was involved in his criminal activities and I still think that. But she lived in the house. She saw everyone coming and going. She should know your suspect and the woman who was with him. They're not my priority. They might come to be part of my case but at the minute they're not. I want to ask questions about the Frate.'

'What's the Frate, sir?' Maxwell interjected.

Maxwell and Gawn had exchanged a questioning look but she had shaken her head. She didn't know either.

'It's what the original group's called. It's Romanian for brother. They regard themselves as a family. That's why we've never managed to get an undercover in among them. They're too closed.'

'Where is Miriam being held and when can I speak to her?'

Gawn was a pragmatist. She didn't think she'd get very far trying to argue with Boyd and, anyway, he was probably right. She might have more chance to get information from the woman. She didn't want to waste another minute.

'She's here in Ladas Drive. And, as for questioning her, whenever you want.'

'Tonight?'

'You want to question her tonight? It's late. We're trying to organise translators and solicitors and so on but I don't think it'll happen until the morning.'

'Doesn't she speak English?'

'Well, yes she does, as a matter of fact. But she's still entitled to a translator if she asks for one.'

'Does she know that?'

'No one has questioned her yet so unless Nuts has her primed with what to expect then probably not.'

'And what about her child? Where is he or she?' she asked.

'Social Services are organising something for the child. It's a girl by the way.'

'She'll probably be frantic about her daughter. It could be a good bargaining chip.'

Gawn saw the look Maxwell cast on her. She could imagine what he was thinking.

'Well then, I suppose you can speak to her whenever you like.'

'We'll be straight over. And, Robert?'

'Yes?'

'Good luck with cracking Nuts.' Gawn laughed. She couldn't resist the joke. For the first time in days she was feeling a bit more hopeful. Would Miriam be able to help them? She could only hope.

Chapter 39

Miriam Florescu looked scared as she cowered on the floor in the corner of the interview room. They were looking at her through a glass panel in the door. Gawn had seen women and men too waiting in terror like that, dreading what lay before them. It was nearly midnight. The woman hadn't seen her baby daughter, Zina, for hours, since the men had come rushing into her house, breaking in the door, shouting and grabbing at her and the others and forcing them down on the ground.

A policewoman had taken Zina from her arms although she had tried to explain that she didn't know anything about anything. She hadn't wanted to play tug-of-war with her child in case she was hurt so she had given her beautiful little daughter, wailing at the top of her voice, into the policewoman's arms.

She had done nothing wrong. She was a good citizen. She told them over and over again. But still they had taken Zina away in a car and forced her to get in a police car too and brought her here. No one had threatened her or hit her. But she was scared. She didn't know what was going to happen to her or when she would see her baby again. Her face showed the lines of tears which she had been crying ever since.

Maxwell had been very quiet in the car while they were making the short trip from one police station to the other. Gawn hadn't seemed to mind. It had given her time to think about how she would approach the interview. Now, just as they were about to walk into the room, he put his hand on her arm to hold her back. She turned to face him, her expression revealing that she had no idea what he was going to say to her.

'You're not going to threaten this woman's baby, are you?'

'Threaten? What do you mean threaten? I wouldn't hurt a child.'

'You know what I mean. A "bargaining chip", Gawn? Really?'

He didn't even try to hide his disgust.

'You'll be in there too, Paul. You can stop me if you think I'm going too far.'

He removed his hand from her arm. She opened the door and walked in.

'Couldn't you get her to sit on a chair?' she snapped at the young constable.

'No, ma'am. Any time I go within ten feet of her she starts wailing.'

Miriam's head came up. Her eyes opened wider. Both Gawn and Maxwell were struck by their vivid violet colour.

'It's alright, Constable. It's not your fault. Maybe you could get us some tea or coffee?' Gawn said.

She took a step nearer the cowering woman and then hunkered down in front of her. Their eyes met.

'Which would you prefer, Miriam?'

The woman looked bewildered and, for a moment, Maxwell began to doubt Boyd's assertion that she could speak English. He didn't know what he had expected but when Miriam did speak he was taken aback. Her voice was shockingly melodic, rich and deep.

'I prefer coffee, please.'

Good. She could speak English, good English with only a slight accent. And she was responding.

'Constable, two coffees and a tea please.'

It was clear that the policeman didn't like being treated like a waiter but Maxwell knew Gawn wouldn't care. Along with the drinks, she would just want him out of the room with his uniform and menacing presence which were obviously unsettling the woman.

'Let me help you up, Miriam. You'll be a lot more comfortable sitting on a chair.'

Gawn reached out and took the woman by the arm helping her stand. She led her to the table and pulled the chair out for her. Miriam sat but no sooner was she down than she jumped up again, backing away from them, looking wildly from Gawn to Maxwell.

'Where's my baby? Where's Zina? What are they doing to her?'

'She's being looked after. No one is doing anything to her.' Gawn was talking to Miriam like a small child using her most soothing tones. 'They won't hurt her. I promise, Miriam. You have my word… one mother to another.'

Gawn's words seemed to have the desired effect for the woman slumped back down into the chair and then just sat sobbing quietly, her tears falling unhindered down her face.

Maxwell looked stunned. He had stretched the truth too sometimes during interrogations; suggested they had evidence they didn't quite have. Every detective resorted to stretching the truth sometimes but to lie about being a mother to win this woman's trust was on another level of deceit in his estimation.

Maxwell turned his attention to Miriam and looked more closely at her. She had a pretty face in spite of the tears. The wisps of hair peeking out from under her headscarf were long and thick and midnight black. Her hands half-covering her face were delicate; the long fingers of a pianist. She had sat back down again but her eyes never left Gawn's face searching for a clue if she could trust her.

'No one wants to hurt Zina or you, Miriam. They'll take good care of her until you can have her back.'

'When? When can I see her?'

Before Gawn could answer, the constable returned with three steaming cups.

'Thank you, Constable. You can leave us now. Ms Florescu hasn't been charged with anything. We're just having a chat. She's going to help us. Aren't you, Miriam?'

No answer. The constable walked out glad to get away from the DCI's disapproving look.

Gawn pushed one of the cups across the table. Maxwell noticed she was still wearing her wedding ring.

'I hope you take milk.'

'Yes. Thank you.' Miriam took the cup and both detectives noticed the tremble in her hand as she lifted it, the liquid almost tipping over the edge.

'Miriam, I'm going to be honest with you.'

Maxwell almost snorted but changed it into a sip of his tea. That would be a change if she was going to tell the woman the truth.

'Things don't look good for you. The people you've been associating with, Danut and his friends, are involved in all kinds of criminal activities. My colleague, Chief Inspector Boyd, will probably want to charge you as part of Danut's gang. They were trafficking women and smuggling all kinds of things into Northern Ireland. You understand? Very serious crimes. You could go to prison. And what would happen to Zina then?'

Telling her the truth. Yeh, go on, Gawn, Maxwell thought to himself. Boyd didn't think she was involved. He had said so. She didn't really believe he was going to charge Miriam. It was another lie to trick her.

'But I never did anything wrong. I am an honest woman.' The woman's voice was filled with anguish.

'Help me, Miriam, and I can help you. I will help you. You'll see Zina again soon. I promise.'

Maxwell wondered how she could sit there and make that promise. Boyd mightn't think Miriam was guilty of anything criminal but she could still be central to his case, an important witness to the comings and goings at the house, and he would want to have her interviewed at length. He would hold her as long as he could.

Gawn took a photograph from the leather folder she had carried into the interview room with her. She slid it across the table. It was the one taken of Hughes and the mystery woman.

'That's your house, isn't it, Miriam?'

The woman didn't speak, just nodded.

'Who are these two people?'

There was only silence. Gawn took a sip of her coffee to cover it.

'I don't know these people.'

Miriam's voice was flat. She was denying knowing their identity but Gawn didn't seem to believe her. If she really knew nothing she would have been much more definite in her denial and for the first time Miriam had allowed her eyes to move from Gawn's face as if she was worried they would betray her.

'They had come to meet with Danut. He must have introduced you to them or told you to expect them.'

Miriam shook her head, vehemently now.

'He never told me anything about his business.'

'But it's a small house, Miriam. You must have heard him talking to them, maybe greeting them when you brought them inside?'

A flash of something crossed the woman's face.

'I think he called the man Edward.' The words were hesitant, unsure. 'But that's all I know.'

'And the woman? How did he greet her?' Gawn had got this much.

Another pause, as if the woman was dredging her memory to help them.

'I think Danut was a little afraid of her.'

'Afraid?' Maxwell said.

This was the first time he had spoken and Miriam looked startled at the sound of his voice as if she had forgotten he was there. All her concentration had been on Gawn. She looked across at Maxwell as she spoke again.

'Danut told me she had connections.'

'Connections?' he asked.

'With the Frate. She had come from Bucharest.'

'She's Romanian?' Gawn asked, surprised.

'No. I don't think so. Danut spoke to her in English and she had an American accent.'

'So you did hear what they were saying?' Gawn pounced on the woman's admission.

'Only when she first arrived. I was closed out of the room afterwards. Danut always shuts me out.'

'And you didn't hear the woman's name at any time?'

'I don't remember.'

'You don't remember whether you heard her name?' Gawn was obviously losing patience. She seemed convinced now, in spite of Boyd's opinion, that Miriam knew more than she was telling.

Miriam began crying again.

Gawn took a deep breath and started over. She was relentless as she fired questions at the woman. Maxwell's sense of discomfort was growing.

'After the two people left, Miriam, did Danut say anything to you? Did he make any comment about them?'

'No. He just told me I would have to go to Belmont and get the house ready.'

Gawn jumped on this mention of Belmont. This was new. No one had mentioned a house in Belmont before.

'What house, Miriam?'

'Danut owns a house there where people stay sometimes when they come to Belfast for business.'

'And you get it ready for him?'

'Yes. I change the bedclothes and vacuum and clean so it is all ready for his visitors. I make it nice for them.' She spoke with pride.

'And you did this for Edward and this woman?'

'I don't know if it was for these people. I only know Danut sent me there straight after they left and told me I must get it done right away. It was going to be used soon.'

'Do you know the address?' Maxwell asked.

'Of course. How could I go there otherwise?'

There was almost a hint of disdain in Miriam's voice and for the first time Maxwell too wondered just how innocent she really was. Did she really know nothing when she had been cleaning and preparing houses for Danut's business associates? Maybe or maybe not.

Chapter 40

They left Miriam sitting over the now cold dregs of her coffee. She would be taken back to a cell and some of Boyd's men would interview her in the morning. Gawn had promised, before Miriam would give them the address, she would check where Zina had been taken and make sure she was alright. And she had kept her word.

'A successful interview, Chief Inspector. You got what you wanted.'

Gawn detected more than a hint of sarcasm in Maxwell's voice as they stood side by side in the corridor. Gawn was stretching her back, her hands on her hips, working her neck from side to side. She straightened up and looked straight at him.

'I got what we needed.'

'By lying.'

'I'm afraid Miriam isn't quite as innocent as she makes out or as Boyd thinks she is. She knows a lot more but it's not our concern so I didn't push it.'

'It was a bit low talking to her "mother to mother".'

'Is that what has you on your moral high horse, Paul? Would you have preferred I threaten her or the child? Maybe make up what could happen to her in prison or what someone might do to her baby in care?'

'No. Of course not.'

'I got the job done, Paul.'

'But lying to her face like that makes us little better than some of the people we have to deal with.'

Gawn knew Maxwell was every inch the family man. Anything to do with children or family and he could be easily upset. She admired that about him but it sometimes blinded him and could be his Achilles heel in an investigation.

'Don't be so bloody naive, Paul. A life is at stake. You do what needs to be done. I learned that a long time ago. Anyway, who says I was lying?'

She hadn't meant to say that but she was angry with him. It was late, her back was sore, she was tired but mostly she was worried. She wasn't sure how much closer they were to finding Jenny Norris, if at all. If anything, this mysterious American woman with connections to Bucharest organised crime only added another level of complexity to the investigation.

If she had slapped him across the face, Maxwell couldn't have registered more surprise.

'You have a child?'

'No. I *had* a child.' Her voice was low. She didn't meet his eye as she explained. 'A long time ago and she was killed. I don't talk about her and it's no one's business but mine. No one else knows but Sebastian and I expect it to stay that way.' Her voice had grown firmer. She looked up then as if daring him to speak of it. 'But when I told Miriam Florescu I knew how a mother would feel if her baby was taken from her, I was telling her the truth.'

She didn't wait for Maxwell to respond. She didn't want his understanding or his pity. She turned away and headed up the corridor.

Miriam had given them an address in one of the narrow streets running from Belmont Road through to Holywood Road in East Belfast. An anonymous location, homes for some older long-time residents and starter homes for couples and little families. A convenient location to live for working in the city centre and famous now for its café culture with almost every other commercial building a café or restaurant. Gawn needed to speak to Boyd urgently to see if his men had raided this property tonight too.

She went straight upstairs, Maxwell hurrying behind her. Before she made it to the Public Protection Branch, she met Boyd in the corridor. He was dressed in a heavy outdoor coat and duncher, obviously on his way out, heading home at this late hour. After his earlier elation, he now just looked tired.

'Robert, we got an address from Miriam for a property at Belmont owned by her boyfriend. Did you raid it tonight too?'

'I don't know anything about a property at Belmont. We've never traced any property there to him and we've never followed him to any property there either. Are you sure?' His brow was furrowed.

'Yes. Miriam says he used it for visitors and he had her cleaning and preparing it.'

'We never put a tail on Miriam. We didn't think she was involved in any of it.' He seemed to be considering what he was going to say before he added, 'Most of my team have already gone for the night. We can raid it tomorrow morning first thing if you have the address.'

'My team's still all here. We could hit it tonight. If word has got out about the others being arrested, anyone in that house may already be on the run.'

She paused and waited anxiously. It was really his operation but she believed Hughes could be there or at least had been there. They needed to act now, not wait until the morning. If they were in luck they might be in time to catch Hughes and his lady friend or if not get some clues left behind in a hasty escape.

Gawn remembered the favour she had done for Boyd and just hoped he remembered it too.

'OK.'

That was all she needed to hear. She didn't wait for him to add anything else. She took off at a run with Maxwell at her heels trying to keep up.

Chapter 41

'All in place, ma'am.'

Maxwell's voice sounded loud through the static on the radio in the quiet of the almost deserted road.

'OK. Give the order.'

Gawn was sitting in her car parked by the side of the Belmont Road outside an old-fashioned newsagent's shop. The building was shrouded in darkness. Looking down the road she could make out the pastel tones of the restored cinema which had been one of her haunts as a teenager and further in the distance the top of one of the giant yellow cranes now synonymous with Belfast. Tonight, she was staying out of the action as she had promised Sebastian. She could do that this time but she knew she wouldn't always be able to or want to hang back, no matter how much he worried.

Even now, in the early hours of the morning, there was some intermittent traffic, an occasional car, some taxis, and even a few pedestrians, groups of unsteady young men or some couples hand in hand. One or two glanced into the car. No doubt they were wondering what was going on, a lone woman sitting in a parked car at this time of night, but as they were using unmarked cars she hoped no one had guessed what was about to happen. She especially didn't want any onlookers with camera phones.

Maxwell was leading the raid. They had cars ready to block off both ends of the narrow street once they were given the word and men stationed in neighbouring streets in case anyone tried to escape over the back walls. An armed response unit was there ready to go in first.

The raid had been hastily planned. Gawn didn't like that. She always wanted to have as much information as possible to know what she was sending her team to face. It might be just an empty house with occupants long gone, warned by some of the others when Boyd's raids had started. Worst case scenario, it could be a group of armed men waiting for them, ready to fight it out rather than be arrested. Or, what she hoped, it could be a sleeping Hughes and his girlfriend blissfully unaware and easily taken into custody.

In the stillness of the night, she heard Maxwell's command, followed almost instantly by the noise of the front door being smashed in. Any second now, she knew she would start to see lights going on in some of the nearby houses. She had already warned Strandtown Station, almost in sight of where she was sitting, and the control room to expect calls from the public about some kind of fracas so they wouldn't waste manpower sending patrol cars to investigate.

'We've got him, ma'am.' Maxwell's voice on the radio sounded more relieved than triumphant. Gawn guessed he too had been worried about what they might have faced when they breached the door.

'Only Hughes?'

'Yes. He was alone.'

'Bring him in. I'll meet you in the interview suite.'

Chapter 42

Hughes looked forlorn. His shoulders were hunched over, a blanket wrapped around them. He looked like a refugee or an old man, badly in need of a shave. His eyes were wild, the eyes of a defeated man, red-rimmed and fearful.

His hair, which naturally tended towards the unruly, was left to hang down unchecked over his face. He was not trying to swipe it back tonight. Rather he was happy to hide behind it. He was almost unrecognisable as the man they had interviewed at Altor Pharmaceuticals.

Now he was wearing only a pair of jeans, slippers, no socks, and a striped pyjama top. They had allowed him time to grab his jeans and put them on before bundling him out of the house and into a car. He had been in his bare feet but someone had retrieved a pair of slippers for him. Now Ferguson and his team were already going over the house, trying to trace the identity of his mystery companion and anyone else who might have stayed there.

Maxwell was waiting for Gawn. She had said she would meet him and he'd expected she would be waiting impatiently for him when he arrived. Instead there'd been time to fetch Hughes a cup of tea and a blanket, and now Maxwell began to wonder where she might be. She had barely spoken to him since their confrontation in the corridor when she had revealed that she had had a daughter. She'd left all the arrangements for the raid up to him. He wondered if she regretted telling him about her child.

He was just about to ring to see if she was coming when she appeared at the end of the corridor.

'Sorry. I wanted to speak to Boyd before we interviewed Hughes. I had to wake him at home and he wasn't best pleased but I've cleared it with him that Ferguson's going to report to both of us. He seems happy enough with that. Actually I think he's a bit embarrassed that they missed the Belmont house in all their weeks of surveillance. Danut must have been very careful to stay well away from there and to cover any traces in his finances about the property.'

Maxwell was about to open the door when she stopped him by stepping in front of him blocking his further progress as he had done to her only a few hours previously. Her eyes locked with his and he thought how beautifully green they were, like deep pools, sparkling now with anticipation of the coming interview.

'Sorry if you think I overstepped the mark with Miriam, Paul. I don't think I did. But no one's perfect. We're all capable of pushing things too far given the right circumstances. Thank you for being my Jiminy Cricket.'

Maxwell looked at her puzzled.

'Haven't you ever seen the film *Pinocchio*? Jiminy Cricket. Pinocchio's conscience. Keep being my conscience, Paul. I know I need it sometimes.'

She smiled at him, then stood back and let him open the door for her.

'After you.' He almost added 'Pinocchio' but decided that might be pushing it so finished with, 'Boss.'

* * *

Hughes lifted his head as he heard the door open. He recognised them and groaned.

'You. I should have known it would be your men who grabbed me like this in the middle of the night from my bed. You've been after me from the minute we met. You want to pin Harriet's murder on me. I know that. I'm not going to answer any of your questions. I want my solicitor now. You can't get away with treating me like this. I'm a respectable businessman. Not some common hood. I was dragged out of my bed half-naked like a common criminal. I was entitled to be there. It's an Airbnb. I've rented it for a couple of nights. I just wanted a break; a bit of peace and no journalists or policewomen hounding me.'

It seemed, for someone who wasn't going to talk to them, he had a lot to say.

'A criminal, yes, but there's nothing common about what you've been up to, Mr Hughes.' She noticed this time he didn't bother to correct her. He wasn't worried about his title now. He had more things to worry about.

Maxwell racked up the pressure. 'You're in deep trouble. People trafficking, drugs, weapons, you name it, your friends are involved in it so that means you're involved too. Up to your neck.'

As Maxwell had been speaking Hughes' eyes had widened. He was shocked. Gawn began to wonder how much he really knew about Danut and his gang.

'If you want a solicitor you can have one of course, that's your legal right, but this is your last chance to talk to us off the record, Edward, and tell us what we want to know so that we can help you. This is your chance to tell your side of the story. Once solicitors are involved any chance of a deal is off the table.' She made the offer and then waited.

The two detectives could almost see Hughes' mind working as he was calculating what he should do. He had no previous criminal record. He was not some hardened criminal who would know that his best defence was to keep his mouth shut and let his solicitor do the talking for him. Gawn's hope was she could get him talking before Hartnett put in an appearance which she was sure he would do. Soon.

'What sort of a deal?' Hughes' eyes darted between the two detectives, fear and panic showing but just a glimmer of hope too.

'Maybe you didn't know your friend Danut was engaged in all these serious criminal activities. Maybe you were just staying at his house as a guest.'

Hughes was nodding vigorously clutching at her suggestion like a man sliding towards his doom over a cliff edge and clinging to a tiny tuft of grass to save himself.

'I'd never met that man before, Chief Inspector. I swear. I had nothing to do with him or anything he was doing. I know nothing about it, any of it. I thought it was just an Airbnb. That's what…'

He stopped suddenly. His voice had been pleading. Gawn wondered what he had been about to say.

'If that's the case,' she said, 'if what you're saying is correct and you can help us, then we might be able to forget some of your involvement.' She made no mention of forgetting his part in his wife's murder.

'What would I have to do? What do you want to know?'

'Tell us how you met Danut.'

He didn't answer right away. After a pause he began speaking, his eyes down all the time, not meeting theirs, examining the top of the table between them as if he would find something to make this all go away.

'Emily took me to meet him. She said he could help us get out of the country. I knew you suspected I'd killed Harriet. I didn't. I swear,' he said looking up at Gawn then and meeting her eye trying to convince her, 'but I knew it looked bad. I panicked.'

Gawn took the photograph of Hughes and the mystery woman from a folder and slid it across the table towards him.

'Is this Emily?'

He nodded.

'And who exactly is she?'

'She's Harriet's half-sister.'

Chapter 43

'Your wife's half-sister?' Maxwell's voice seemed an octave higher than normal. He had not been expecting that. Neither of them had.

'Her name's Emily. Emily Madson. She's a… friend… and a business associate. She's going to invest in my new company.'

Suddenly Gawn realised that was why she had seemed familiar. Face on, she would probably have made the connection between the two women right away but with only a partial side view she had merely evoked a feeling of having seen her somewhere before.

Then she had a eureka moment, as her old boss in the Met had called them. It was not Harriet Hughes she had seen at the window on Monday night. It was not Harriet Hughes who hadn't wanted to speak to her and hadn't answered the door to her knock. It had been Emily Madson and suddenly their timeline was all awry. Harriet may well have already been dead when Gawn was at the bungalow. She might have been killed earlier, much earlier, when Hughes was there.

Gawn took a second to compose herself before continuing the questioning.

'Tell me about Emily.'

'I found her on a family history site.' He saw their puzzled looks and went on, 'Harriet was adopted. You didn't know that?'

'We haven't been able to get her birth records from America yet. We're still waiting for them,' Maxwell responded, not wanting to let the man think they had missed an important fact in the case.

Gawn scowled at him. Hughes didn't need to know that. He needed to be telling them things, not the other way round.

'I thought you'd have discovered that.'

His look moved between the two detectives. He wanted to win their trust.

'She was born in a little town called Bisbee in Arizona down near the Mexican border. When she was just a few months old she was adopted by a couple who were working out there. I don't know how official the adoption was. Harriet didn't either. But they were well-off and Harriet always suspected they might have paid her birth mother for her. They couldn't have children of their own, you see, and were a bit old for an official adoption. That's what she suspected anyway. She never knew her birth mother nor anything about her although her parents did tell her she'd had an older sister. The Wrights, her adoptive parents, moved back to England when she was about five or six and Harriet never learned anything more about her sister.'

'And Emily?'

'I didn't even know she existed for sure. Harriet thought she might have died. Emily was three years older than her. I was just trying to find some relative, maybe a cousin or something. Then I found Emily or rather she found me. She told me her story. She was never adopted. She was taken off her mother and ended up living in foster care and then group homes until she was old enough to fend for herself. She ran away from the last one when she was fourteen. She told me all about it. It was horrendous. All the things she went through.'

'And what about her birth parents? Did Emily trace them?'

'She never knew who her father was. All the foster care records were lost in a fire. That's why Emily put her DNA on the website, hoping to find some relatives.'

'How did Harriet feel about having a sister?'

'She didn't know about her until last Monday.'

'You told her on Monday? Was that what you argued about?'

'Yes.'

'Was Emily at the bungalow last Monday night?' Gawn asked.

'I think so.'

'You think so.'

'I told Harriet about Emily on Monday night and we had a row. She guessed we were having an affair.'

'And were you?'

'Yes.' He had lowered his head and lowered his voice too. They could barely hear him. 'Harriet didn't love me anymore. She wanted a divorce. Emily was so like her in some ways. It was like being with Harriet when we were, you know… but she was totally different in other ways. Harriet was quiet. She'd always been submissive.'

Gawn had to prevent herself reacting to his use of the word 'submissive'. In her interpretation, he meant he'd been able to do what he liked to her, beat her about and she had never fought back until, with Jenny's help, she'd got up the courage to leave him.

'Anyway, Harriet wanted out of our marriage and she was prepared to let me use the money from the sale of our house to help me set up my company. I had hoped she might give me some more money to help me. After all she had plenty and she said she'd consider it. Then I told her about Emily and we had the argument. A stupid argument. She would have come round. She always had before. But she attacked me and we struggled and she stumbled and fell and hit her head on the table. I panicked when I saw the blood but I swear she was still alive when I left.'

Harriet attacking Hughes seemed very out of character. Gawn didn't believe him. The rest might be true but not that Harriet had attacked him. Maybe she had defended herself for the first time?

'Where was she when you left?'

'In the living room, sitting in an armchair. But she was alive, I swear.'

'What did you do then?'

'I was freaking out. I phoned Emily and told her what had happened. She said to leave it all to her. She would see Harriet and explain everything.'

'And then what?'

'I went home.'

Before Gawn could ask another question, the door swung open and Jerome Hartnett strode into the room looking angry.

'I sincerely hope my client is not being questioned without his solicitor present.'

'We were just having a friendly chat, Mr Hartnett. Your client hasn't been charged with anything.'

'Has he been cautioned?'

'Not yet. It was just a chat while we were waiting for you.'

He cast a withering look at her.

'We're interested in his friend, Emily Madson. That's who we were talking about.'

Years of watching faces during interrogations meant Gawn could read the solicitor's face too. The name Emily Madson was not new to him. She couldn't even have explained exactly how she knew. The merest flicker of his eyelids, a slight dilation of his pupils, a furtive glance towards his client? But she knew. Hartnett knew Emily Madson or at least knew of her.

'I would like to consult with my client in private now. He will not be answering any more questions tonight.'

Chapter 44

It was past two o'clock in the morning. They had waited but Hartnett had refused to let them question Hughes any further, and until they had more than circumstantial evidence against him they were in danger of having to let him go. He had admitted fighting with his wife but he had not been under caution at the time and he had had no representation so good luck with getting that to stick. Even then, he had denied killing her. All they had against him so far was his association with Danut, but if he stuck to his assertion that he had merely rented a house from him for a few days, they were not going to be able to hold him and once he was released he would run.

There had seemed little point in going home. She decided to try to get a few hours' sleep in her office. She had sent Paul home and the others were gone too, just a skeleton night crew in place. She had sat with a mug of coffee beside her. Probably not the best thing to be drinking but she was so tired she didn't think it would keep her awake. She wanted to jot down some ideas before allowing herself some sleep. That was where Maxwell found her, head resting on her arm on the desk.

He looked amazingly fresh for someone who had only had a few hours' sleep but he had been in his own comfortable bed and he'd been able to have a hot shower and some breakfast at home before appearing. She didn't know what she must look like but she did know what she felt like. She tried to stretch to get some feeling back into her arm where her head had been resting on it. She pushed her hair back off her face and Maxwell saw the scar at the edge of her hairline again, an ugly reminder of an ugly time in her life. He had heard vague stories about how seriously injured she had been in Afghanistan. They had gone the rounds when she was first appointed but she never spoke of it and he was never brave enough to broach the topic.

'You look rough, boss.'

'Thank you, Inspector. Make a woman feel good, why don't you?' But she smiled at him appreciative of his concern.

'Here.' He held out a cup of coffee.

'Lifesaver. Thank you.'

She stood up and stretched and took the cup out of his hand. She took a sip and then asked, 'Right, where do we start today? Updates on the BMW?'

'Nothing. No sightings.'

'Then I think we pull everyone off that. Leave it to ANPR and hope we catch it somewhere. We know Jenny wasn't driving either car. We know some man was. We just don't know who he is yet. Maybe it was Danut. That's possible. We can get Boyd to check if they had him under surveillance then or if he could have been at the bungalow. In the meantime get them to run facial rec and see if they can match the man in the car to Danut.'

'Is there any chance Danut was the man you saw with Harriet in the John Hewitt?'

'The American art lover?' She hesitated but only for a second. 'No. I don't think it was him. What about Lyons and Ferguson? Have they turned anything up?'

'They've been working all night. They've lifted quite a few prints and they're running them through the various databases.'

'And what about Hughes' phone? We need to corroborate what he told us about who phoned whom and when and get a number for Emily Madson; see if we can trace her through it.'

'We're waiting for the service provider to get back to us. Apparently, according to Hartnett, Hughes lost his phone yesterday.'

'How convenient.' Gawn's voice was dripping with sarcasm.

'We could try talking to Hughes again.'

'Not without his solicitor present,' she said. 'He made that very clear last night or rather this morning. And I value my job and yours too much to try to interview Hughes without him there. We'd have to have something very definite to offer to make him cooperate. Hartnett won't let him talk to us without a good offer on the table. And even then, maybe not. He's wily. He might think Hughes' best chance is to say nothing, that we'll never get enough to prove he killed Harriet, and he could be right. Maybe it wasn't him.'

Maxwell looked at her.

'You've changed your tune.'

'There's a lot more to this case, Paul, than just an argument between a husband and wife getting out of hand. I'm not sure yet what it's all about but I do know that much. I don't like Hughes and I don't trust him but I think he's way out of his depth. Anyway we don't have anything to offer him until we know how Boyd's investigation is going and if he can link Hughes to any of Danut's activities.'

'I'd be pretty sure he isn't involved,' Maxwell said. 'Did you watch his face when I was talking about people trafficking and gun smuggling? He was practically shitting himself.'

She sighed.

'Where is Jenny, Paul? Is any of this stuff with Danut anything to do with her or have we just got totally sidetracked now?'

She ran her fingers through her hair and Maxwell noticed she was still wearing her wedding ring. She caught his glance at her hand.

'I'm not ashamed of being married to Sebastian. That's not why I chose not to wear my wedding ring. I just didn't want my marital status to become a distraction but I guess I can't hide it forever.'

'Understood, boss. No comments. But don't be surprised if a few of the team congratulate you when they notice the ring.'

She nodded. So long as that was it, a nine days' wonder, she could cope with that.

'Back to business. Right. I've been thinking about what Jenny could have got herself involved in. That text she got telling her to bring something with her.'

'Yes?' Maxwell waited for what she was going to say.

'Well, she'd hidden the flash drive, hadn't she? It was very deliberately hidden. I didn't find it. Surely that must have been what they wanted? What else could it be?' Gawn asked.

'And by "they" you mean this Emily Madson woman, whoever she is, and the man who was driving Jenny's car?'

'Yes. Get on to the American authorities. We need more information about Emily Madson. If she has links to the Frate as Miriam said, she almost certainly has a police record. Do we believe she really is Harri's half-sister? She certainly looks a bit like her, enough to fool me so I thought it was Harri I was seeing at the window. And she told Hughes to leave Harri to her and she ended up dead. I think we have a new prime suspect.'

Chapter 45

Maxwell had checked for an update on the flash drive.

'They've got it open, ma'am,' he informed Gawn.

She looked brighter at his news. She had taken time to have a quick shower and to don the change of clothes she kept in her office for just such an occasion as today. Her auburn hair was shining and she'd applied a thin touch of make-up to put some colour into her cheeks. She felt more alert and ready for action.

'They've sent across a copy.'

'Let's have a look at it then. Have you looked yet?'

'No. I was waiting for you.'

He sat down at his computer and clicked the file open. A page of numbers and cyphers appeared before them.

Gawn was hovering behind him looking over his shoulder.

'What the hell is it? I was expecting details of a bank account, maybe something to do with money laundering or some incriminating video or something from a case Jenny had been involved in,' Gawn said.

'But it was Harriet's secret. Not Jenny's. She was only keeping it for her friend, remember?'

'So, what is it?'

'I'm no expert but could it be a chemical formula or maybe something scientific, a bit like the stuff Hughes had up on his wall,' Maxwell suggested. 'Remember all the notes and stickies?'

'Yes. I remember. So you think this could be something to do with him rather than Danut's activities?'

'Well, I don't know, boss, but it would make more sense, wouldn't it? It could be linked to whatever Hughes was working on, this test he's supposed to be developing. But why would his wife have it and why would she ask Jenny to hide it for her?'

'And why was someone prepared to kill her to get it?' Gawn added.

'I guess we need to find someone who can tell us what this is.'

'I think I know just the person,' said Gawn, 'and, if he can't, I'm sure he'll know someone who can.'

'Who?'

'One of Seb's friends from the university. Aaron Chalmers. He's a professor of Biomedical Sciences. Seb introduced us at a party. I'll see if he'll meet us today.'

Chapter 46

Two hours later Gawn and Maxwell were sitting on hard plastic chairs in a corridor in the Medical Biology Centre at the university, waiting for Chalmers. The place was eerily empty, only a few keen students about. Distant noises echoed down the long corridor.

A distinguished-looking middle-aged man in a white lab coat approached them, his footsteps echoing loudly. His face broke into a smile as soon as he saw them and he began speaking before he reached them, his voice booming through the empty space.

'Gawn Girvin-York, how lovely to see you again, my dear. And without that reprobate of a husband of yours hovering around in case someone tries to spirit you away.'

He gave a hearty laugh, obviously pleased with his own sense of humour and the opportunity to compliment her.

'Aaron, thank you so much for seeing us at such short notice and agreeing to help.'

When Chalmers came alongside them, Maxwell was surprised when he placed both hands on Gawn's shoulders and planted a kiss on first one cheek and then the other. It was obvious he regarded her as a close friend. Whether she reciprocated, Maxwell doubted. He had never seen a huggy-kissy side to his boss. He didn't think she had one.

'Always delighted to be of service to the police, my dear. And especially to you, of course. I always aim to help damsels in distress. How is that old rogue of a husband of yours by the way? You can tell him I'm missing our games of squash, missing kicking his ass.' He laughed his hearty laugh again.

'He's fine. He's taken up surfing now instead.'

'Ah, becoming a real Californian beach bum, eh? He won't want to come back to this dreary old country after all that sunshine. Now, let's take a look at what you've got, my dear. Come on in.'

Maxwell noticed, although she had tried to hide it, that Gawn had flinched when Chalmers had mentioned Seb not wanting to come back. He wondered if she was worried about that, if that was what had been playing on her mind recently. It wouldn't be surprising if it was. Belfast didn't have quite the cachet of LA or the possibilities for Seb's career either.

'By the way, Aaron, this is my colleague, Inspector Paul Maxwell.'

'Paul, good to meet you. So you're the lucky man who gets to work with this lovely lady every day.'

Gawn looked embarrassed.

Chalmers unlocked his office door and led them inside. The interior immediately reminded Maxwell of York's office in the university the first day they had met him, except the skeleton hanging in the corner of the room and the specimen jars of human organs sitting on a shelf were rather different decorations to Seb's choice of artwork.

'Here's a copy of the USB.'

Gawn handed it across. Chalmers pointed them to a squashy sofa in the corner and then inserted the USB into his computer. He sat down and they watched his face as he opened the document and studied it carefully for several seconds, his head moving from side to side as his eyes followed the writing on the screen. They could see the light from the computer monitor reflected in his glasses.

'You said on the phone you thought this could be something to do with a test for Huntington's?'

'Yes.'

'There are already various tests, you know. And this isn't one. I have no idea what it is. Sorry.'

Chapter 47

It quickly became apparent that Aaron Chalmers liked the sound of his own voice and enjoyed being listened to. He was used to having a captive audience of admiring young students. Although they hadn't asked for it, he began with an exposition on Huntington's disease, much of which they already knew. A quick internet search had provided their limited knowledge, as much as they needed for the purposes of their investigation. However, they didn't interrupt him, just listened politely, waiting until he got to the bit that interested them.

'It's caused by an inherited defect in a single gene. And it can develop at any time of life, at any age, even children, but most often the first symptoms are noticed in people in their thirties or forties.'

Around Harriet's age, thought Gawn. Had she had Huntington's? That might explain Hughes' interest in the disease. No. Munroe would have noticed at the PM. He wouldn't have missed that.

'Progression can be slow so it's possible to live with the disease for a long time. But any treatments we have at the minute can only postpone the inevitable.'

Gawn was getting impatient. They hadn't come for a lecture.

'What if you knew someone in your family had the gene, is there some kind of test like amniocentesis you could have done?'

'There are genetic tests. But potential carriers are always counselled so they understand the implications of getting a positive result and of course there's always the possibility of using in vitro fertilisation with pre-implantation testing so only eggs without the gene are implanted as an alternative.'

IVF. Seb had already mooted the possibility that this was something they might consider depending on what the consultant in Dublin told her.

'So tests do already exist?'

'Oh, yes.'

'So why would Hughes be getting excited about developing a new one?'

'I don't know, my dear. It's hard to see what advantage there might be to any new test unless it was going to be significantly cheaper or something. Now, if it was a treatment which could repair or replace the rogue gene, well that would be a game-changer. But, as I said, what you have here is not a formula for any test.' The professor was adamant. 'If you think this relates to genetic testing, you're wrong. It looks more like…' He paused and then went on more slowly. 'I'm no expert but this looks more like the formula for some amphetamine and a pretty potent one at that.'

'You mean the drug?' Maxwell asked.

'That would be my guess. And as for all these other numbers, I have no idea at all what they mean.'

'But I know a man who will.' Gawn turned and looked at Maxwell. 'We need to talk to Hughes again.'

Chapter 48

Monday, new day, new week. And a new Hughes too so it seemed. They'd had to wait until the morning to speak to Hughes. Hartnett had insisted. Now he was looking much more like the man they had first met. He had shaved and his hair had been carefully brushed. His solicitor had obviously arranged for some clothes to be brought for him so he was dressed in a dark suit. With the clothes some of his confidence had returned as well.

Gawn and Maxwell walked in silently. They didn't greet either man. Gawn took the flash drive out of her pocket and placed it on the table in front of Hughes without saying a word. He reacted as if she had set a bomb down in front of him. He moved back, scraping the legs of his chair on the floor.

'What is this?' Hartnett's smooth voice asked.

'Dr Hughes knows. Don't you?' Gawn turned to Hughes and fixed him with a stare.

'No.'

She pulled out a printout of the page from the USB and set it down in front of him.

'What about this? Look familiar?'

She slid it across the table but he turned away from it. Instead Hartnett reached out and picked it up. He scanned it for a few seconds and then let it drop casually back onto the desk.

'What's this all about? What exactly is my client being accused of now? First you're questioning him about murdering his wife. Then it's some tilting at windmills allegation of being involved in people trafficking because he happened to have rented a holiday home owned by some criminal. And now there's this, whatever it is.'

Hartnett reached across again and pushed the page towards them disdainfully.

'Dr Hughes knows exactly what it is and he knows how it's got two people killed already,' Gawn said.

'Two?' Hughes was shocked.

'Who else has been killed, Chief Inspector?' Hartnett asked.

'A petty criminal called Frank Campbell who was sent to retrieve this flash drive,' she said.

'And is my client supposed to have killed him too?' Hartnett sneered.

'I doubt it. The man was killed because he failed to find this. Dr Hughes' friends were looking for it but now we have it. Our people will find out exactly what it is and then we'll see what your client has been involved in.'

'I don't know what it is, what all those figures mean,' Hughes blurted out. 'She asked me to keep it for her and then the stupid bitch found it and wouldn't give it back.'

Hughes ran his hand through his hair almost pulling at the roots in his distress.

Gawn thought she was following what he was saying but she could see from both Maxwell's and Hartnett's expressions that they didn't.

'She, being Emily Madson?'

'Yes. She needed it kept safe, she said. People were looking for it, she said. She didn't tell me who but they were trying to get hold of it. It was worth a lot of money.

That's what she said and she asked me to look after it for her. She was going to sell the information and I would get a share, enough to start up my business.'

'What sort of information?'

'I don't know. I told you. I never tried to look at it. Never opened it. I just put it in my briefcase. I thought it would be safe there. And then Harriet must have taken it out. She probably thought it was something she could use against me in the divorce. Maybe details of my finances or something. I don't even know when she took it. She could have had it for days. I didn't notice it was gone until Emily asked me for it and it wasn't there. She went fuckin' crazy then. I thought she was going to kill me. She had a gun. She pointed it at my head.'

'So you told her Harriet had it?'

'Yes.'

'And then what?'

'She told me to get it back so I went to see Harriet last Monday night to beg her to give it back to me.'

'Not about mortgage papers then? Or blood samples?'

'No.' Hughes almost laughed. 'Not about mortgage papers or blood samples.'

'And what happened?'

'I need to speak with my client before he answers any more of your questions,' Hartnett said. 'We'll take a break, Chief Inspector.'

Hartnett had been strangely quiet during the exchange. Gawn had been expecting him to intervene at some point so she was not surprised, just annoyed, when he brought her questions to an end. But that didn't stop her face looking like thunder. She felt they were so close to getting important information that would help them find out who had taken Jenny and why. Hartnett was closing the door in her face… again.

Chapter 49

While she waited for Hartnett to talk to his client, Gawn made her way back to her office. She spent thirty minutes sitting at her desk, seething. It was frustrating that she hadn't been able to question Hughes any further and now she wanted to talk to Maxwell and plan their next move. She noticed two new pictures on the murder board as soon as she walked into the squad room.

One was the side-faced view of the woman they now knew as Emily Madson. The other was of a man. He was olive-skinned with a shaven head and deep-set eyes. It was obviously a police mugshot. Who was this, Gawn wondered. McKeown was standing waiting for something to come off the printer and, as if she had been reading Gawn's mind, she piped up.

'Alex Ruiz, ma'am.'

McKeown lifted a sheet of paper which had just worked its way out onto the printer tray. She glanced at it.

'Blimey,' she said. 'Ruiz has quite a rap sheet.'

Gawn was about to reprimand her for her use of the Americanism, but before she had the chance to, the sergeant handed the page to her. Gawn's eyes scanned down taking in the list of charges this man had faced or was facing. Bank robbery, home invasion, rape and homicide. He was a career criminal… and a very dangerous one.

'One seriously dangerous villain but how does he end up on our board, Erin?'

It wasn't her sergeant who answered but Maxwell who had come out of his office when he saw her arriving.

'They found his fingerprints in the bungalow. It was good work. Lyons says they've lifted a lot. They eliminated the victim's own. They've already identified Hughes' prints in the living room and the hallway but that doesn't really help us because he admitted to being inside the property. It'll take days to run all the rest but Lyons started with the ones they got in the hallway to see if he could identify our arsonist. Ruiz's showed up on the front door.'

Gawn walked past Maxwell into his office. He followed her and closed the door behind them. The fingerprints showed Ruiz had been at the bungalow. Had he murdered Harriet? And, if he had, where did Jenny come into it all? Had she walked into the middle of the attack and been murdered too? If so, where was her body? No, whoever had been there had moved Jenny's car and taken her away, dead or alive. To do what with her? The only thing she could think of was the flash drive. They wanted the flash drive. Jenny held the key to them getting it. Campbell had been sent to search her apartment and hadn't managed to find it.

All these thoughts whizzed through her mind. And then she realised Ruiz had been the man in the John Hewitt with Harriet, the American interested in buying her artwork. He looked different of course with his hair long and in a ponytail but Gawn was certain it had been him.

'Ruiz is no minor thug, Paul. He's a major criminal. What in God's name is an American killer doing in a bungalow in the middle of the countryside in County Antrim? What had Harri Hughes got herself involved in? And how did Ruiz even get into the country? The Americans are looking for him.' She waved the page she was holding in her hand. 'Have you seen this, Paul? No, of course you haven't. Here. Look at it.' She thrust the page towards him. 'He's wanted by the FBI. Why did he come here? And how did he end up at Harri's? What the hell was going on?'

She dropped down into an armchair and ran her fingers through her hair. She bit her lip as she watched Maxwell, who had been reading the page, carefully taking in all the details. She saw his expression grow more and more serious.

'We'll have to alert upstairs. They need to know. If we have an American serial killer on the loose they need to know. It's bigger than just our case,' he said.

But they never got the chance. Maxwell's phone rang and he answered it.

'Yes, sir. Yes. She's with me now, sir. Yes, I'll tell her, sir.'

He put down the receiver.

'That was Reid. He wants you right away.'

It wasn't often Chief Superintendent Reid spoke to her directly. Usually she was called before McDowell to pass on the reprimand for whatever she had done to upset the senior officer.

'I don't think I've done anything that would get me in his bad books.'

She couldn't think why he would want to speak to her unless he knew about her personal involvement in Harriet's murder case and thought she should have recused herself, or unless he already knew about Ruiz and she couldn't think how he would have found out so quickly.

'He didn't sound annoyed,' Maxwell said. 'More like he was… under pressure.'

'Then I suppose this means they already know about Ruiz somehow.'

Whatever his reason for wanting to speak to her, she wasn't going to keep him waiting.

Chapter 50

'Come in.'

'You wanted to speak to me, sir?'

Gawn addressed the balding figure seated behind his cluttered desk. A flash of white caught her eye and she half-turned to see a well-dressed Eurasian man sitting in an armchair in the corner of the large office. He stood up politely unwinding himself from the chair. He was tall, very tall. Well over six foot six with broad shoulders and a slim athletic build which accentuated his height. His hair was short, cut in a style which immediately made her think 'military'. He had teamed his white button-down collar shirt with a midnight blue suit and finished it off with a tie whose motif she recognised instantly as that of the Special Forces Green Berets. He might as well have had 'American' tattooed across his forehead, she thought.

'Chief Inspector, this is Special Agent Patrick Takenaka of the FBI.'

She half-smiled at him, wanting to appear friendly but secretly concerned at this development. Thoughts were flying through her brain. The FBI doesn't operate outside the United States, at least they weren't supposed to. She had heard there was an international team which was called upon when Americans were the victims of crime abroad but that wasn't the case here. Harriet Hughes had been a British citizen according to her passport which they had now managed to get hold of. It was the CIA not the FBI who spun their web worldwide popping up wherever America's interests dictated. The suspicion crossed her mind that Takenaka could just as easily be CIA and she didn't like that thought at all.

He walked across the room and extended his hand to her, a generous grin lighting up his face. She had to admit to herself he was an impressive specimen of a man, handsome in that rugged film star sort of way that appealed to some women. And solid. One hundred and eighty pounds of prime American beefsteak, as she'd once heard one of her army colleagues describe an American working alongside them. She could see him playing the role of one of those spy heroes in the films she knew Maxwell liked to watch. His grip was firm but he was careful not to press her hand too tightly. His hands were soft and smooth. He probably moisturized, she thought to herself. He let go making sure not to hold on to her hand overlong but his eyes, which held an amused gleam, lingered on her face.

'Chief Inspector Girvin, I'm delighted to meet you in person at last. I've heard of you, of course. We have some mutual friends, I believe.'

When he spoke, his voice deep and mellifluous suggested a laid-back character. But Gawn had never met a Green Beret yet who was anything other than hyper-vigilant and always ready for action.

At his mention of mutual friends, images came into her mind. She didn't want to go there, especially with Reid listening in. If they had any mutual friends, they were the kind of men she had tried very hard to forget.

'Sit down.' It wasn't an invitation from the chief superintendent. It was an order.

Takenaka, with impeccable manners, pulled the chair out for her and kept his hand on the back while she sat. Then he retook his seat beside her.

'Special Agent Takenaka wants to share some information with us which might impact your case, the Hughes murder,' Reid continued, his obvious awe at having an FBI agent in his office causing Gawn some amusement.

She tried to show no surprise at his words. They had only just found out about Ruiz and a possible American connection to the case. Takenaka had been very quick off the mark. How had he got here so quickly? And what did he want?

'If you'll allow me to explain, Chief Superintendent?' He paused for a fraction of a second but it was obvious he wasn't really asking for Reid's permission to speak. 'Chief Inspector, a red flag came up on our system late yesterday evening when someone here ran some fingerprints which link to our Most Wanted List; two people we're very keen to get hold of.'

Two people. She kept her best poker face on. Who was the other person? She realised it had to be Madson.

'The prints belonged to Alex Ruiz. He works with a woman called Megan Sloan. At least that's one of the names she uses. They're wanted for murder in several states. We already knew they were in Europe and probably heading to Ireland from intel and chatter we'd been monitoring. That was what our information led us to believe. We tracked them as far as Romania where we knew they had connections with a criminal group called–'

'The Frate.' Gawn wanted to let the American and the Chief Super know she was ahead of them.

'Yes. The Frate. Very good, Chief Inspector. I'm impressed.' He smirked.

Supercilious bastard, Gawn thought to herself. Did he think they were a bunch of hicks?

He bowed his head to her in acknowledgement. She didn't react but noticed her boss seemed pleased.

'We were sure they would head over here so I was in Dublin waiting. When I got the call from Washington about the fingerprints I got a flight to Belfast this morning.'

Gawn tried to keep her face absolutely blank but it was becoming more difficult by the minute. How on earth American villains on the run from the FBI factored into

Harriet Hughes' murder and Jenny's abduction, if that was what it was, she couldn't even begin to guess.

'I'd like to work with you on this.' Takenaka smiled at her, ignoring Reid as if he had no say in the matter. 'Obviously I have no jurisdiction here in the UK.'

Gawn almost raised her eyebrows when he said that. It had never stopped others in the past although she supposed that was more the CIA than FBI but she was sure Takenaka had every intention of interfering in her case no matter what he said.

'I hope we can cooperate. I can certainly provide you with information about Megan Sloan and Alex Ruiz and that should help you find them and solve your murder case.'

'Emily Madson.'

'Sorry?'

'Emily Madson. That's what she's been calling herself here.'

In the game which she felt she was playing with Takenaka that was at least deuce, she thought. Reid, sitting like an umpire midway between them, beamed. Almost match point to the PSNI, his face seemed to suggest.

Madson or Sloan or whatever her real name was must have been in the house too. They just hadn't identified her prints yet. She had told Hughes she would take care of Harriet. So she and Ruiz had suddenly taken prime position in the hunt for Harriet's killer and Jenny's abductors.

Collaborating with this man was the last thing Gawn wanted to do. His priority would be capturing the two Americans; hers was getting Jenny Norris back safely and then catching Harriet's killer. But it wasn't really down to her. If Reid agreed then she'd have to go along with it.

'Of course,' said Reid. 'We want to offer every assistance to our fellow law officers, and we'd be glad of any information you can provide. Isn't that so, Chief Inspector?'

She knew what she was supposed to say so she said it. 'Of course, sir.'

Chapter 51

Reid had offered a few more platitudes about inter-agency cooperation and teamwork and then told her to take the American and introduce him to Maxwell and the others. Then they could all get started working together. He had beamed as he shook Takenaka's hand.

As she led the lanky American along the corridor and down one flight of stairs to the Serious Crimes offices she didn't offer any casual conversation and she had no intention of chatting about any mutual friends. They walked side by side in silence but she was aware Takenaka was watching her. She found herself wondering who exactly their mutual friends might be and what he had been told about her. But she hadn't time to worry about that now. She was still trying to get her head around his sudden appearance in the middle of her investigation. She needed more information about Madson and Ruiz. Did their involvement make it more likely Jenny was still alive or more likely she was already dead? She felt she was at a disadvantage with Takenaka and that made her uncomfortable.

Every eye in the room turned towards them as they walked in and then quickly went back to their work. Maxwell was already standing at the door to his office, prepared to greet them.

'Inspector Maxwell, this is Special Agent Takenaka of the FBI.'

She could see Paul's eyes light up. He was obviously not immune to the glamour of the world-famous crime agency either.

'Call me Patrick, please.' The American was mounting a charm offensive.

'I'm Paul.'

Gawn hoped he wasn't going to be dazzled by years of watching TV shows and movies about the glamorous side of the FBI.

'Let's sit down,' Gawn said, 'and get down to some of this collaboration Chief Superintendent Reid is so keen on.'

Gawn hadn't intended her voice to sound quite so harsh. She didn't like being blindsided or having to work in the dark and she didn't like having to collaborate with outsiders, outside her control. She didn't trust Takenaka. She didn't trust anyone outside her team.

'I can understand you're not particularly keen having someone come and muscle in on your case, Gawn. May I call you Gawn?'

He asked but he didn't wait for her reply. She knew then he wasn't lying about mutual friends. He had pronounced her name correctly to rhyme with Dan, not making the mistake usually made. Someone had told him about her; someone from her past.

'I can assure you I have no intention of doing that,' he said. 'I want Sloan and Ruiz caught. If you can do it, that's great. I just don't want them to get away again. They escaped from us once. We had them but they shot their way out of the local jail with a little help from the outside. They're not going to do it again.'

Gawn saw Maxwell's puzzled expression at the mention of the name Sloan. She needed to catch him up without giving the appearance of knowing nothing much about how the two American fugitives were linked to her case.

'Let's go over what we know so far.'

Gawn took them through what they had discovered – most of it, not all.

The American listened carefully, sitting back, legs crossed, elbows resting on the arms of the chair and his fingers steepled up to his mouth, almost as if he was praying. He nodded from time to time.

'So this guy Hughes is a geneticist? That explains a hell of a lot. Sloan – sorry, the woman you know as Madson – believes she suffers from Huntington's. Have you heard of it?'

'Yes, of course,' Maxwell said.

'It's incurable. Sufferers begin to experience some of the symptoms in their thirties and forties.'

Gawn was afraid they were going to be treated to another lecture.

'Yes. We know all about it,' she interrupted him, her impatience showing.

'Right. Well, Madson started to develop some symptoms which she diagnosed for herself as Huntington's and then went searching for her natural parents – she was brought up in foster care – and for cures. She's tried quite a few, especially some of these clinics in South America that take your money, pump you full of natural herbs and promise you a cure. At the last one she went to, when it didn't work as she thought, because she still had the symptoms, she killed her doctor. She's indiscriminate in who she kills. No favourites.' A wry smile played on his lips.

'And Ruiz?' Maxwell asked.

'He's her partner in crime. They're lovers. He's the alpha male, the muscle, but she's the brains. They went on a crime spree in Arizona, after the episode in Mexico – two home invasions and five dead from two different families. In one family, the father was a geneticist, like your Dr Hughes. The other family was the social worker who placed Sloan into care and eventually into a group home where she was raped at age ten. Payback, I suppose.'

'So you think she came here looking for a cure from Hughes?' Gawn asked.

Some ideas were forming in her mind but an explanation as to how it all tied into a formula for an amphetamine type drug seemed to remain just out of her grasp.

'As far as we've pieced together from our electronic monitoring, Hughes put DNA on a database some months back,' Takenaka explained. 'Sloan made contact because her results matched his wife's. She knew they must be closely related. Sloan's crazy. She blames the care system for everything that happened to her. She never knew her father and her biological mother was a high school dropout, a junkie. The mother OD'd on drugs in the end but Sloan was taken off her when she was about five. With no parents to blame I guess she blames her sister. She was old enough to have vague memories of her as a baby. The sister got out and by all accounts seems to have had a pretty good life. Her adoptive parents were well-off.'

And that was where Harriet would have got the money, Gawn thought.

'Sloan carried a photo of herself and her sister together when she was about two and her sister was just a baby. She showed it to the FBI agent who was questioning them when we caught them. She was fixated on it. One got a lovely life, your Harriet Hughes, and she didn't. Cue revenge.'

The image of the black-and-white photograph in Hughes' office flashed into Gawn's mind. She stood up suddenly.

'We need to talk to Hughes urgently. He could be in danger, couldn't he? Madson and Ruiz might be after him now. Or he could be working with her. This could be just what we need to get him talking.'

But they were too late. Hughes had been released pending further inquiries.

Chapter 52

Maxwell remembered reading once of someone being incandescent with rage but until now he had never actually seen it. Now he knew what it looked like. Whatever had been said, she set the receiver down carefully on the desk and clenched her hands into fists. Maxwell had never heard her swear much before. Normally she kept her feelings under tight control. But now he imagined she was dredging out of her memory every expletive she'd ever heard. When she had calmed down a little, she picked up the receiver again.

'So you're telling me he's been released? Seriously? How did it happen?'

She was on the phone in his office. She'd had Grant escort Takenaka to her office to wait while she contacted the custody suite to have Hughes brought to the interview room… or so she had thought. Instead, as Maxwell had realised from her side of the conversation, she had been informed that Hartnett had demanded Hughes be charged or released on bail and with the limited evidence they had, McDowell had taken the decision to have him bailed.

She slammed the phone down.

'What did McDowell think he was playing at?'

Maxwell wondered if it would be wiser to stay quiet or to try to support the superintendent.

'I suppose Hartnett didn't give him any choice. Charge him or let him go pending further inquiries. We do it all the time, boss.'

'Don't be so bloody reasonable, Paul. I don't need you to explain. I need you to be as annoyed as I am. Just because we do it all the time, doesn't mean he should have done it this time and he should have asked me or at least told me first. We might have got some more information to charge Hughes for all he knew.'

Maxwell was annoyed and worried too about what this move meant for Jenny Norris' chances of survival. But he didn't think ranting about it would do any good.

'But we don't, do we, boss? We have no new evidence against Hughes at all. And McDowell hadn't even been told about our new suspects. If he had, he would have been even more likely to have him released. These two look very good for it. And Hartnett probably put a lot of pressure on him,' Maxwell argued.

'I should go and speak to McDowell.'

'And say what exactly? Throw your career away? Have a bit of sense.'

She knew he was right. Going to McDowell and venting her anger at him would only see her taken off the case and suspended and that would do Jenny no good at all.

'Our one hope is that he remembers enough of real policing to have put a tail on Hughes.'

She didn't really expect it but she had to hope.

Chapter 53

Gawn realised Superintendent McDowell would have known, even as he was issuing the order for Hughes' release, that she would be livid about it. But when she calmed down she realised Jerome Hartnett would have left him no choice.

When McDowell phoned her and explained he had ordered a tail on Hughes she accepted it without comment. Ruefully he had then explained how the tail had lost him. Hughes had left in the passenger seat of Hartnett's car into heavy traffic heading towards the city centre. The two officers in the following car had been held up by an elderly woman in a little red Skoda entering the yellow grid at the junction of Newtownards and Albertbridge Roads, blocking the way just long enough for them to lose sight of the silver Mercedes as it sped citywards. When they caught up, Hartnett was just pulling into a business park opposite a church near Bridge End and when he got out of the car, they could see there was no one else inside the vehicle. Hughes was gone.

* * *

'So we've had to let our main suspect go,' Gawn was explaining to Takenaka.

'I thought the police here could question people for a couple of days.'

'We need to bring charges or at least be able to prove why bail isn't appropriate while we carry out further investigations. I guess Hughes' solicitor convinced my boss that Hughes wouldn't interfere with any ongoing investigation and wasn't a flight risk.'

'Really?' Takenaka's tone of voice grated on her. She might think McDowell was an idiot but she'd defend him to the American.

'So is it more likely Hughes has gone on the run *with* Madson and Ruiz or he's running *from* them now? He seemed to be really scared of her when we questioned him and he told us she had a gun.'

Gawn was thinking aloud, something which she always enjoyed doing with Maxwell. Takenaka was there too but he seemed happy to sit back and leave them to it, offering only the occasional comment.

'I want every patrol car on the lookout for him.'

'Do they pick him up if they see him, boss?'

She hesitated before answering and looked across at Takenaka.

'No. If he's in league with Madson he could lead us to her. If we pull him in and question him, he could just stonewall and leave her enough time to escape.'

'And if he's not, he could end up as target practice for her,' Maxwell suggested.

Gawn's response was immediate. 'Worth taking the risk.'

Maxwell almost said, it's not your life you're risking, but decided not to challenge her, with the FBI man there.

Takenaka stood up.

'So I guess it's just a waiting game now,' he said. 'Look, I'm going to check in at the consulate, let them know what's going on and then freshen up at my hotel. I guess you'll let me know if you find Hughes or where Madson and Ruiz are hiding out.'

There was a sardonic smile on his face. She guessed he was well used to unhappy cops who didn't like the FBI coming in and trampling all over their case. And no doubt he was feeling suitably superior at the bungling cops who had let their main suspect go.

'We'll let you know if anything breaks,' Gawn assured him, knowing she would leave it until the very last minute to have everything sorted before he could get there.

'I'll head back to my hotel then. You know where I'm staying. So, you'll let me know if there are any developments?' Takenaka said as he stood. 'Unless you'd like to have dinner with me this evening while we wait, Gawn?'

'Sorry. I have other cases to supervise. I'll be busy this evening catching up on them,' Gawn said.

It wasn't true, of course, and he would realise that. Gawn didn't care. She didn't want to have dinner with him. She didn't really want to eat at all and the thought of sitting, making pleasant conversation or trying to exchange reminiscences about their mutual friends held no appeal.

Takenaka took his leave.

Gawn and Maxwell stood and watched as Jamie Grant escorted him out, the American towering over him. Grant would no doubt pump him for stories of the exciting cases he had been involved with. It would make his day.

Chapter 54

'So now we wait,' Maxwell said and sat back in a chair putting his feet up on the coffee table.

'Like hell we do. You heard the man. These two are cold-blooded killers. If they took Jenny they could kill her at any time without giving it a second thought.'

She walked over to the door, swiping his feet off the table on the way past. She opened it and shouted across the room.

'Find Edward Hughes. Now. He can't just have disappeared.' Then she turned to Walter Pepper. 'Walter, I want you to use some of your charm. Find out where exactly Harriet Hughes was born and where her adoption took place.' She saw McKeown's head pop up at the mention of adoption.

'I want to know everything about her life, her adoptive parents and especially her natural parents. Whatever's closed in the case files, get it opened. Do whatever you have to, to get the information we need. Don't take any confidentiality crap. This is a murder case and other people could be in danger. And find me exactly where Harriet got her money from. And, Erin, see what else you can find out about Madson's crimes.'

'Yes, ma'am.'

'But Takenaka's already told us all about the adoption and we have their arrest sheets,' Maxwell pointed out looking puzzled.

'We find out for ourselves.'

'You don't trust him?' the inspector queried.

'I don't trust anybody outside this team. Our super agent has his own agenda. You can be sure of that.'

Gawn glanced across at the murder board. Another photograph now filled the space alongside Harriet's. It was a picture of Madson or Sloan. Both names were written underneath it. The family resemblance was clear.

Maxwell was standing directly behind her. She turned round to him.

'Where's the report on the victim's clothes?' she asked.

Maxwell turned to his desk and rifled through a pile of papers finally picking one out and handing it to her. She flicked through it, scanning the information.

'I wish I'd checked this sooner or seen the victim's body.'

She remembered that Harriet's body was already being removed by the time she got there. It was Maxwell who had been there earlier and given permission for it to be taken away.

'Why? I saw the body. There was nothing to see except her head wounds.' Maxwell was confused.

'Because it was Madson I saw on Monday night, not Harriet, and I might have realised that sooner if I'd seen the body. I should have stopped them on Tuesday and insisted on viewing it. That was my mistake and it might cost Jenny her life. Look, Harri was wearing a dark shirt. It's here in the list of clothing. But the woman I saw at the window, the woman I waved at, was wearing a light-coloured jumper, yellow I think. I didn't know Harri that well. I'd only met her once, briefly. It was Madson who was at the window, not Harri. Harri was probably already dead when I was there. Remember Munroe put the time of death from 8pm onwards. She could already have been lying up the lane. I might even have seen her if I'd looked around a bit.'

'In which case they'd have killed you too. So you think they were there when you were outside?'

'Probably. Yes.'

'Then what?'

'Hughes had fought with Harriet but he hadn't managed to get the flash drive back. Madson had told him she'd clear up his mess. So she and Ruiz must have gone to the house.'

'What about Madson?'

'She hated her sister. Remember what Takenaka said about her profile? She wanted her sister to suffer like she had. I wouldn't be surprised if it was Madson who chased Harri and struck the fatal blow rather than Ruiz.'

'You didn't tell Takenaka about the USB.'

'No. I didn't.'

'But we know Madson gave it to Hughes for safe-keeping so it's something to do with her.'

'Yes.'

'So shouldn't we have told him?' Maxwell asked.

'If it's something she's involved in, Takenaka already knows about it. But he hasn't shared that with us, has he? He probably doesn't know we know about it. I haven't had time to update McDowell yet.'

'Are we playing games, boss?'

'Saving Jenny's life is no game. But that's what the FBI and CIA are best at.'

'You think he's CIA?' Maxwell was shocked.

'Maybe. Maybe not. What I do know is that his priorities are different to ours. I'm running this case my way, not his. We need to find out what the stuff on the USB is about. It didn't belong to Hughes. Madson gave it to him. It's something to do with her. We need to solve it. How are you at puzzles?'

'I'm not bad at jigsaws.'

'Come with me.'

Chapter 55

Maxwell didn't know this area of South Belfast well. Gawn drove past Forestside's upmarket shopping centre and headed out of the city. He wondered where they were going. She hadn't told him anything, merely ordering him to get his coat and come with her.

They followed a Translink bus lumbering up a steep street and bouncing over the sleeping policemen jolting its passengers. He recognised a well-known pub, its car park full with the lunchtime clientele, and then at a roundabout she drove straight ahead, seeming to be heading further out into the countryside. At the last minute she turned into a quiet estate of houses and bungalows. The roadway was narrow, never designed for the number of cars parked at each house.

Eventually she stopped in front of a neat, detached house which looked no different to any of its neighbours except for the car sitting outside. Maxwell recognised the yellow Ferrari taking up all of the short driveway. He would have liked to ask her who they were going to see but, as she hadn't volunteered any information at all on the drive here, he held back.

'Come on.'

She climbed out and walked to the front door. By the time he had joined her, she had already rung the bell and was waiting for the door to be opened. They could hear barking and high-pitched yapping from inside. The door opened and a shaggy-haired young man dressed in T-shirt and jeans stood holding on tightly to a huge Irish wolfhound.

'Charlie, down,' he said. 'Get down!'

The dog's head was huge. The dog was huge. Yapping with excitement around Charlie's feet, but small enough to run backwards and forwards underneath his body, was a small black pug.

'Gawn. This is a surprise.' The young man opened the door even wider. 'Come in. Let me get this door closed and these two crazies inside.'

He laughed and backed into the hallway dragging the wolfhound behind him while the little dog followed.

'I'm sorry to arrive without warning, Cathal. I need your help.'

The man's eyes moved past her to take in Maxwell standing looking bewildered behind her.

'Sorry. This Is Paul Maxwell. Paul, this is Cathal Cunningham.'

If this was meant to explain anything, it didn't. Maxwell had never heard of Cathal Cunningham.

'Hi, Paul.'

'Cathal was a student of Seb's in Berkeley. He's a computer whizz and a bit of an all-round genius.'

Cunningham looked embarrassed at her description of him. He would have looked about eighteen if it wasn't for his thick bushy beard and some touches of grey in his hair which suggested he was older. He didn't look like a genius but then Maxwell didn't know what a genius was supposed to look like.

'I'm serious. He's in the top one percent of people in Britain, he's a computer expert and he loves puzzles, don't you, Cathal?'

***

Cunningham took them into his study which was at the back of the house. A bank of computers, reminding the two detectives of Hughes' office, was ranged along one wall, their screens filled with scrolling lines of code. Gawn had explained their situation briefly and then produced a flash drive from her pocket.

'This might take a while,' he said. 'Do you want to make yourselves some coffee? You know where everything is.'

They left him to it. Maxwell looked back as he shut the door and saw Cunningham, headphones on, already tapping away at one of his keyboards totally focused, oblivious to everything else.

'Tea, Paul?'

Gawn was in the neat, little kitchen. She had made her way there without hesitation. She'd obviously been here before. Maxwell noticed the expensive coffee machine sitting out beside a supersized American fridge. Kerri had suggested buying a coffee maker just like this, even though neither of them were great coffee drinkers. Apparently they were trendy. She had shown him a picture in one of the home interior magazines she loved. He might have agreed until she told him the price.

'Yes. Thanks.'

He watched as his boss got boiling water from a tap. This guy liked his expensive gadgets. She made Paul a mug of tea and herself an espresso showing a familiarity with the machine which suggested she probably had one herself. It wouldn't surprise him.

'So, you know this guy through Seb?'

'Yes. Seb was his tutor at Berkeley. Cathal was studying History then but he developed an interest in computers and he did his doctorate in that. But by that time, they'd struck up a friendship – two Belfast boys far from home, I suppose. When Cathal turned up here again and set up his own computer company, he got in touch. They play poker together every week. Sometimes Seb comes here, sometimes Cathal comes to us so I've got to know him too.'

Maxwell realised he knew so little about this woman who he had worked alongside for three years. But he had learned a lot in the last few days.

* * *

They were sitting at the kitchen table. Maxwell was down to the dregs of his tea; Gawn was on her second espresso when the door opened and Cunningham sidled in looking pleased with himself. Gawn thought he looked like DC Grant, innocently delighted at his own cleverness but without any conceit.

'Sorted,' he announced.

'You've decoded it?' she asked.

'It wasn't difficult; not sophisticated at all. It was a mixture of numbers and hieroglyphs.'

'So what is it?'

'Well, it doesn't mean anything to me but maybe it will to you.'

He handed a page to Gawn. She looked carefully at it.

'Right. There are a lot of numbers but at least they're in some sort of order now,' she said. 'I think from their configuration they're dates, the American way round. And these could be amounts of money. That would be my guess. But these other numbers' – she handed the page across to Maxwell – 'I have no idea. We'll need to look at it more closely. And these names mean nothing to me. Some seem to be people and some… I don't know. New Mexico Warriors. Is that a baseball team?'

Maxwell shrugged.

'You've done your bit. Thank you, Cathal. You've been a great help. Now all we have to do is work out what it all means and that's our bit.'

'Anything for you, Mrs GY. I'll let The Man know you were here when I'm speaking to him later.'

'You'll be speaking to Seb tonight?'

'Yeh. We're playing online poker later. Shall I give him your love?' he teased.

'I'll do that myself. But thanks, Cathal. This is really useful.'

Chapter 56

'If these are dates, they're all in the next few weeks.'

Maxwell was leaning over a printout of the page Cunningham had decoded for them the day before. He took another chocolate biscuit from an opened packet on his desk and dipped it into his tea in an unconscious movement. He didn't usually do that at work and Kerri didn't like him doing it at home either. She said it made him look common. He was an inspector now and this was only the beginning as far as she was concerned. She was much more ambitious for him than he was for himself.

Gawn was standing at the back wall of his office. She had just pinned a map up on his noticeboard over the top of messages about a mental health initiative and a staff rota and was running her finger over it. Maxwell had never seen a map like it before.

'Are you going to explain what that is, boss?'

'It's a US Census Bureau statistical map. The numbers we have on our list are GEOID codes. They refer to the state, the county and so on right down to subdivisions.' She pointed to the different columns of numbers.

'Here. Move over.'

She sat down at his computer. She had been working until the early hours at home, calling friends and ex-colleagues on both sides of the Atlantic. She felt she knew what this was all about now and why the USB was so important. She typed in 'US Census Bureau statistical map' and a number of interactive maps came up. She chose one and zoomed in on an area in Arizona, then clicked. Up came a 14-figure reference.

'That number pinpoints that exact spot on the earth's surface using the USA's earth coordinate system based on their satellite technology. What we have are ten of those sets of figures,' she said.

'So ten places where something is hidden.'

'Or going to be handed over or where a meeting is going to take place. The beauty of this is it can be out in the middle of nowhere but if you have the technology, you can go directly to the spot.'

'How do you know all this, boss?'

'I'd like to say I had a sudden brainwave but it's not true. I used the search engine on the computer. I put in the first line of numbers and up came the map with the information. Second set of numbers, the same and so on. If you have the map and the numbers you can find anywhere in the US down to within a few metres.'

'Blimey.' Maxwell was impressed.

'I found the maps online but I didn't know the rest so I phoned an old friend of mine from my army days. He works for ICE now. He does a lot of work along the southern border tracking illegal immigrants and smugglers. I explained what we had and he told me the rest. Smugglers use these references for pickups for their contraband or where they leave off people being smuggled across into the States. So, in essence, we have ten of these locations along with dates and the names of individuals or groups like the New Mexico Warriors – which is not a basketball team, by the way. It's a biker gang with a nice line in drug dealing. And this.' She pointed to another name on the list. 'They're a militia group in Arizona. My contact told me that too.'

'And these figures?' Maxwell asked.

'My guess, it's money. Very large amounts of money but if this is linked to drugs, especially some new potent type of amphetamine, it would be worth a lot of money.'

'So what do we do now? Do we tell Agent Takenaka and give it to him?' Maxwell asked.

'No. This information was important enough to bring Madson and Ruiz to Europe and for her to have Hughes hide it for her. She was prepared to kill to get it back, although I suspect Harriet's murder was as much personal revenge as anything else. They killed Campbell when he failed to get it back for them and they'd already taken Jenny.'

'Doesn't that mean it's likely Jenny's dead too?' Maxwell spoke gently, suspecting that was what she had probably been thinking and afraid of how she would react to his statement.

'Yes. It probably does.' Her voice was even quieter than his. She bit her lip before speaking again. 'But we haven't got a body yet and until we do I'm working on the premise that she's still alive.'

'So, back to my original question, boss. What do we do now?'

'We find Hughes. He's the key. If anyone can get a message to Madson, it's him. If he can contact her and tell her he has the flash drive, we can get confirmation that Jenny is still alive and then we can set a trap.'

Chapter 57

Erin McKeown was looking puzzled as she walked into Gawn's office.

'What can I do for you, Erin?'

'You asked me to try to get you some more information on the Madson and Ruiz crimes.'

'Yes. So, what have you found?'

'It's what I didn't find that has me puzzled, ma'am. I looked in the local papers for the areas where the crimes took place. We had the dates and the addresses and the details of the victims so I thought I would read up what had been reported at the time locally. It might give some more detail or comments from witnesses or whatever. Just something extra.'

'And?'

'Nothing.'

'What do you mean? You didn't find anything we didn't already know?'

'No. I mean nothing. Literally, nothing. There was nothing reported about those murders. The papers were full of all kinds of stories. Minor stuff even. In Bisbee a concert in the local elementary school took up a whole page with lots of photographs – this was on the day after the murder of a geneticist and his wife and daughter so you would think three members of a family being slaughtered in their own home might make it into the paper.'

'Maybe the reporters weren't very on the ball and it wasn't reported for a couple of days. Some of these tiny local papers only come out once a week, you know.'

Gawn's mind was going into overdrive.

'I looked online at seven days of local papers. Every paper I could find, and the regional versions of the bigger papers too. Two days before and four days after. For both murder scenes. Nothing.'

'Maybe the dates were wrong,' Gawn commented but she was thinking furiously. The FBI wouldn't make a mistake. No, two mistakes like that.

'So I rang the local sheriffs' offices.'

'And?'

'I think they thought I was spoofing them or something. I was some mad woman putting on a funny accent and making stuff up. They didn't seem to know anything about it at all.'

Gawn's face revealed her confusion. What was going on? Takenaka had turned up and the rap sheets had conveniently appeared to explain his presence. But from the very beginning she had been suspicious. What if he was after Madson and Ruiz for some other reason? There were lots of murders every week in the USA, lots of multiple killings, gangland, even serial killers. The FBI pursued them but they had enough to do looking for them inside the country without sending a special agent halfway across the world following them around Europe.

Gawn's old boss in the Met said she had a built-in radar for bullshit and this was what she sensed now. Takenaka was after the USB. He had created a whole story about a crime spree. It would have been easy for him to fabricate the police records which would be triggered when a search was carried out on their names but he mustn't have had time to create a backstory and doctor more documents to support it. It had probably been a rush job and anyway he was too arrogant thinking they wouldn't check it out. He'd been wrong. She hadn't trusted him from the beginning. Now she knew exactly where she stood with him.

Chapter 58

What Hughes did next surprised them all. Maxwell had issued his photograph to the airports and ferry terminals as well as the main train station. They had men asking at the local car hire firms too. He and Gawn expected Hughes to flee, get out of the country. Instead, with two forensics officers still working in his house, he had opened the door and walked in surprising them and himself too. They immediately brought him in for questioning.

'How dumb can you be?' Maxwell asked as he and Gawn watched Hughes on a monitor. 'He went home. It must have been like something from a comedy film. I don't know who would have been more shocked. Hughes or our two guys.'

'I think he really must be a bit of a dupe in all this. He was just being used,' Gawn suggested.

'Do you think he'll help us?'

'Keep your fingers crossed… and your mouth shut.'

He looked at her with a hurt expression on his face.

'This is one time I don't need Jiminy Cricket on my shoulder.'

* * *

Mouth already quivering, Hughes watched as the two officers walked in. They sat down facing him. No word was spoken but Gawn had not taken her eyes off his face.

'No beating about the bush, Edward. We haven't time for that. The Americans might arrive at any minute.'

'Americans? What Americans?' Hughes looked wildly from her face to Maxwell's, then to the door.

'Don't tell me you've never heard of extraordinary rendition? Guantanamo Bay?' She let her words hang in the air.

'Quantan… what are you talking about? What's going on?'

'You tell us. The Americans want that USB. I don't know what's on it. Must be something to do with their war on terror and you were the last person to have it.'

'No! No I wasn't!' He was shouting. 'Harriet had it and that friend of hers. She had it.'

'Jenny Norris?'

'Yes.'

'How do you know that, Edward?'

Hughes looked towards the door. He would be expecting his solicitor at any minute or the Americans. Gawn banged her fist down hard on the table making both Hughes and Maxwell jump.

'Hartnett can't save you, Edward. By the time he'd even get a High Court judge to listen to him, you'd be halfway across the Atlantic in an orange jumpsuit. We're your only hope.'

She watched his eyes. They were darting around the room. He seemed to make a sudden decision.

'Emily told me. After I left on Monday night Harriet told Emily that her friend had it.'

'So Emily Madson was definitely at Harriet's on Monday night?'

He nodded.

'And then what?'

'I didn't hear anything more until after Harriet was dead. Emily phoned and told me it had been an accident. She told me to go back to the house on Tuesday morning and set a fire. I panicked. I didn't want you to know I'd been there on Monday night and Harriet and I had had sex and then we'd fought over that stupid USB and she hit her head. I knew it would look bad. Then, when you questioned me, I knew you thought I'd killed her. I phoned Emily again and told her. She said to wait but after you questioned me again and I came up with that stupid excuse about the blood, she arranged for me to go to that man's house.'

'Danut?'

'Yes. Him.'

'But you'd already been at his house before – on the afternoon before your wife died.'

'Emily needed to pick up some documents or something from him. That was to do with her. Nothing to do with me.'

'So what was the plan?'

'I was to stay at Belmont and wait to hear from her. Emily was going to wait around until the heat was off. That was what she said. Then the Norris woman was going to tell them how to get the USB.'

It was a glimmer of hope. Just that. Hughes might be lying but she didn't think so. Madson might have lied to him but at least there was still a chance Jenny might be alive. But Gawn couldn't understand why they hadn't just tortured the information out of her and killed her. She was a liability.

'Jenny Norris is still alive?'

'Yes. At least she was the last time I spoke to Emily. They still hadn't got the USB. The Norris woman told them she'd given it to her friend but the friend was away for a few days in Dublin and she wouldn't be back until today. She offered to phone her and arrange for it to be handed over. That's all I know about it. I swear.'

Hughes looked from Gawn to Maxwell before speaking again.

'I know you don't think much of me, Chief Inspector. You've made that very plain but I'm not the monster you think I am. I never meant for anything to happen to Harriet. I didn't set out to cheat on her with Emily. God, I didn't even know Emily existed until a couple of months ago. Now I wish I'd never met her. I didn't know she was such a fuckin' psychopath. She used me. I'm a victim here too.'

He started to cry. Gawn didn't have time to listen to his self-justification and she wasn't going to waste any sympathy on him either.

'What do you expect from me, Edward?'

'I want to help you. Help you to find Emily. Make some of this right.'

His eyes were wide open like an excited child, waiting to hear how she would respond, still hopeful that things could be turned around; that everything wasn't as bad as he feared.

'Can you phone her?'

'I don't know her number.'

'But you phoned her before.'

'She put the number in my phone but she told me to throw it away as soon as we'd finished speaking. She said she would contact me. She gave me a new phone and said she would phone me when she had everything ready for us to leave.'

'Do you know where she is?'

'No.'

'Do you know where she would go?'

'No. I suppose she'll try to get to America but God knows how. She never told me any details.'

Gawn stood up, convinced he was wasting her time now. He knew nothing more. Nothing that could help her.

'But I do know she can fly,' he blurted out, realising he was losing her.

'You mean, fly a plane?'

'Yes. She has a PPL. From when she was living in Florida. And I heard her speaking to someone on the phone and talking about renting a plane.'

If – and it was a big if – she was going to try to fly out, that would cut down the places she could be. There were a few small airfields up at the north coast and in Fermanagh but the nearest one was in Newtownards less than fifteen miles from where she was standing now and on the edge of Strangford Lough where Jenny's car had been scuttled.

Chapter 59

'Right. Listen up, everyone.'

Gawn was breathless from running as she rushed into the room and spoke loudly to make sure she had everyone's attention.

'We've got a lead. Emily Madson can fly a plane. A thirty-minute flight and she's in Scotland, England or wherever she has enough fuel for. Erin, get on the phone to Newtownards airfield and see if they have any private planes there owned by or leased to a woman answering

Madson's description and, if they have, are there any flight plans for a journey soon. Jack, you do the same with St Angelo and, Jamie, Eglinton. If we don't turn up anything at these, then we'll try City and International but I think she'd be more likely to go for a small airfield. Less formality. Fewer questions asked.'

Gawn began pacing waiting to hear back from the three detectives. She knew it was a long shot. Even if Madson was going to fly herself out, she might have a small plane hidden somewhere and take off from a field.

Gawn was like a tiger in a cage. She had been holding everything in for so long and now she needed to be doing something. She couldn't have stayed still unless someone had tied her to a chair. No one approached her. They kept well away. Even Maxwell didn't try to start a conversation.

Dee was the first to put the phone down. He looked across at her and just nodded his head.

'Right. Right. Thank you, and that's this evening?' Erin McKeown was finishing off her conversation and it was clear she had some news.

'They have a Citation CJ3 leased for three days,' she said. 'It can carry up to six people and has a range of about 1,500 miles. The man I was speaking to said it was leased by an American called David Minchkin. He also said when Minchkin called in yesterday to sign for everything, he was driving a dark BMW.'

'Has he filed a flight plan?' asked Maxwell.

'Yes, sir. Round trip to Southampton. Over this evening and back the day after tomorrow.'

'Except they'll just disappear once they get to England. And no one will investigate until the plane doesn't reappear in Newtownards giving them a day's head start. After that, who knows? What time are they due to take off?' Gawn asked.

'Seven o'clock.'

She looked at her watch. It was just coming up to three o'clock.

'Right, get the whole team into place on standby. If it comes to it, we can substitute some of our people for the airfield workers. Better have ARU there too. We know Madson and Ruiz aren't averse to using guns.'

Now she was in her element. She was never happier than when she was in the thick of the action.

'And get on to the traffic cams in Newtownards. See if we can spot the BMW and trace where it went after it left the airfield yesterday. Get the chopper on standby. It would be better if we could intercept them before they reach the airfield. And they definitely mustn't get as far as the town.'

Chapter 60

'It's you, isn't it? Jenny was talking about you.'

Gawn and Maxwell were in her office. Gawn nodded.

'She didn't give you a copy of the USB, did she? That's not something else you've kept from me?'

'No. Of course she didn't. She never gave me the USB, never even mentioned it to me.'

'Then why all this story?' Maxwell was trying to understand what was going on.

'I think she was trying to buy herself some time,' Gawn suggested.

'For what?'

'Time to have a chance to escape. Maybe. Or just to stay alive. Or time for us to find her. She'd know someone would be looking for her… probably me. That's all I can think of.'

'So, what now?'

'I guess, we wait. We keep doing everything we've been doing to try to find Madson and Ruiz and meanwhile we wait and hope for a call from Jenny.'

'You think they'll let her phone?'

'If they want the USB badly enough and she's convinced them I have it and know nothing about what is on it, then yes.'

* * *

They waited. They drank cups of tea and coffee. They listened to negative reports coming in. No one had any information for them. Madson and Ruiz had gone to ground. They'd managed to find the BMW but then lost it as it travelled towards Greyabbey on the coast road outside camera range. It could have turned off anywhere. Searching could take days and they only had hours, if that. The pair could be anywhere, even out of the country already, if Gawn's idea that they planned to fly out, was wrong.

And then they waited some more.

Gawn had gone to her own office. She said she needed time alone. Eventually, just after four o'clock, she walked back into the squad room. She thought she probably looked as if she had aged ten years in a few hours.

'Nothing?' she asked but she didn't expect a response. If Maxwell had heard anything he would have let her know straight away.

Then her mobile vibrated in her pocket. She pulled it out and looked at the screen.

'I don't recognise the number. Did they get the trace set up on it, Erin?'

'Yes, ma'am.'

She took a deep breath and pressed the button.

'Yes?'

Gawn couldn't help her face revealing it was Jenny Norris on the other end of the phone.

'Hi Jenny. I didn't recognise your phone number. Have you changed it?'

They had decided, if Norris did phone, she would pretend to know nothing about her being missing, expecting that Madson would be listening in. She had to work very hard to keep her voice casual and as normal as possible.

'Lost it? Typical you … Yes, I just got back from Dublin this afternoon … I had a great time. You should have stayed too. What have you got up to while I've been away?'

Maxwell watched her face as she was obviously listening to her friend's reply.

'The USB? … Of course I still have it … You want me to do what?'

She was listening carefully.

'Well, it'll be a bit of a rush but I think I can make it … It sounds a bit weird … How will I know him?'

Another pause while she listened.

'Will you not be there?'

Pause.

'OK. Well, we'll have a drink later tonight then. I'll call over to your apartment after eight. See you later, for sure.'

As soon as she finished the call, she looked at McKeown.

'No good, ma'am. Not long enough for a trace and it's switched off now.'

'Damn.' Gawn hadn't really expected it would be as simple as tracing the call. Madson wouldn't make a silly mistake like that.

'Well, what have you got to do?' Maxwell asked.

'I've to bring the USB to Albert Mooney's.' She had named a popular bar and restaurant in East Belfast not far from Police HQ. 'Someone will be there to take it from me.'

'How will you recognise them?'

'They'll recognise me, apparently.'

'When do you have to be there?'

'In half an hour.'

'God, that doesn't give us much time to get anything set up.'

'I would imagine that's the idea, Paul.'

Chapter 61

By 4.25pm, they were all in place. Just. It had been a crazy rush. McKeown and Dee were seated in the restaurant area in Albert Mooney's trying to look like a couple on a date. They were still trying to catch their breath after a quick car dash and run in from the car park to pretend they had been sitting over a meal. They had gone right to dessert to give the impression they had been there for a while. Their table overlooked most of the bar area.

Grant was sitting in a window seat at a fast-food restaurant directly across the main road, his Ulster Rugby beanie pulled down tightly on his head. He was aiming to make his chips and burger last as long as needed, picking them up one by one and chewing them slowly. He looked uninterested but his eyes were constantly on the move watching all the comings and goings, missing nothing.

Logan was perched on a bar stool looking like a man in serious need of a drink but whose half of Guinness stood untouched in front of him. Other members of the team were sitting in cars in the side streets nearby, the bus lane preventing them from stopping on the main road. They were ready to follow whoever picked up the USB no matter which direction he went. Grant's foot was jiggling with anticipation. McKeown and Dee, whenever their eyes met, looked, not like a couple in a romantic relationship, but anxiously at each other.

At 4.30 exactly Gawn drove her Audi into the familiar car park behind the bar. She manoeuvred it into the last free parking space and got out. Evening was already setting in. As she walked through the narrow laneway towards the main door, she realised it was much darker and hidden from view than she had remembered it. She wondered if they intended to jump her before she reached the bar and steeled herself in readiness but nothing happened. She made it safely inside.

The bar was busy. It always was. She scanned around as if looking for a friend. Neither Madson nor Ruiz were here. At least she couldn't see them. She was about to walk over to the bar when a young man in jeans and a motorbike jacket approached her. She looked intently at him but he walked past without a word. Then in her peripheral vision, she was aware of an unshaven middle-aged man in a dark leather jacket standing up from his armchair at the window and moving across to her.

'You have something for me?'

She had expected a foreign accent, possibly one of the Romanians who hadn't been arrested, but this man spoke in a broad Belfast accent.

He held out his hand. Gawn took the USB from her pocket. She whispered something in his ear as she handed it over. She hoped he'd understood her message.

'Don't follow me,' was all he said in response, ignoring her comment.

He turned abruptly and walked out. Gawn had to fight the urge to chase after him. She had to trust her team. Logan was already making his way out past her having watched the exchange reflected in the mirror over the bar. McKeown and Dee were talking to a waiter, making their excuses for leaving. They walked past her as well without a second glance. After the longest twenty seconds of her life, she walked out and back to her car.

Chapter 62

Reports started coming in immediately. A car was ready to tail the target but he had crossed the main road at a pelican crossing opposite Grant in the fast-food outlet. Because he was on foot, Maxwell ordered Grant to follow him.

The man walked up the main road past a block of little shops and a stretch of school railings and took a right turn into a wide avenue lined with detached homes. The street was empty. No traffic. There was no one else walking in the street apart from the target and Grant. Maxwell ordered the detective to hang back and then peel off as if he was calling at one of the houses. They had a car waiting on Kings Road at the bottom of the avenue. It would take over.

Kings Road was narrower, darker, tree-lined. The houses here were older and even larger, well set back behind high hedges. No one was on foot here. There was never much foot traffic on this road except in the afternoon when the green-uniformed girls from the nearby school laughed and chatted as they meandered out making their way home. The two officers in the car let the target get well ahead until he reached a bend in the road and was almost out of their sight. Then they started up the engine and drove past him and into the car park of a church at the next junction. Here they were able to sit and watch as he walked past. He wasn't hurrying. He wasn't looking around him.

'He's crossing the main Knock Road, sir.'

'Where the hell is he going?' Maxwell's disembodied voice sounded worried, as worried as Gawn was feeling as she listened in on the radio as she drove back.

'No matter what, we can't lose him,' she ordered.

'Shit. He's met someone. At the entrance to the Greenway down the side of the old people's home. I think it's Ruiz. They're talking. He's just passed something to him. It must be the USB. Now he's walking on towards Castlereagh.'

'What about Ruiz?' Maxwell queried.

'He's gone down the Greenway.'

'One of you get out and follow on foot,' Maxwell ordered.

'We'll have to hang back a bit, sir. There's nowhere to hide. He'll make us right away if we get too close.'

The Comber Greenway was a cyclists' and walkers' domain, no traffic. It was part of a cycle network and followed the route of the former railway line from Belfast to Comber. Popular during the day with dog walkers, it was unlit and little used at night.

'He's got a moped. Hidden in the hedge.'

'Damn!' They'd never be able to keep up with him. 'Get cars to all the possible exits to the Greenway,' Maxwell ordered, but even as he spoke, he knew it was impossible. The man could make his way off the Greenway anywhere along its seven miles through gardens or even the cemetery. They were going to lose him and lose the USB.

Chapter 63

They did lose him. His escape route had been well planned. They would have needed an army of men to cover all the possible exits and air support too and there just hadn't been time to get any of that organised.

When Gawn walked into the office, Maxwell was standing looking both angry and distraught – angry they had lost their target, distraught he had failed Jenny and Gawn too.

'Anything?' she asked.

'They got the moped. Abandoned at the cineplex. There's a huge car park there. He could have had a car or someone waiting to pick him up.'

'What about the man who took the USB from me?'

'We got him. He's in the interview room. I've had a word with him already. I thought he might be able to tell us something,' Maxwell answered her.

'And was he?'

'Not really,' he admitted.

'Who is he?'

'His name's Davy Wells. He has a bit of a record for petty crime. Nothing serious. He claims he was slipped a few quid by an American in a bar to get the flash drive from you.'

'And what about the man he passed it to?'

'Positive ID. It was Ruiz. So they've got the USB and they've got Jenny and she's no more use to them now.'

Before Maxwell could tell her how sorry he was he had let her and Jenny down, Gawn's phone rang.

'Yes. Good. Let me get a pen.' She took a pen and a piece of paper and jotted something down. 'Erin, get the ARU and all the team to these coordinates asap.'

'Yes, ma'am.'

Maxwell was upset. Gawn had put him in charge of setting up the tail while she had been doing God knows what. She hadn't shared with him what she was doing. All his plans had failed. They would kill Jenny for sure now if they hadn't already. He felt the guilt for her death heavy on his shoulders. But when he looked at his boss she didn't seem despondent. He knew that gleam in her eye. He had seen it before.

Gawn walked past him into his office and beckoned him to follow her. She closed the door behind him.

Chapter 64

'I made a deal with the devil, Paul.'

'What? What are you talking about?'

'While we were waiting for Madson to get in touch, I contacted Takenaka. I always knew it was possible we'd lose the USB. They had days to plan any handover.'

'So what did you do?'

'I gave them a version with only some of the information on it.'

'You mean, it's no good to them?'

She nodded.

'But they'll kill her… if they haven't already.'

'It was always a possibility that as soon as they got the USB, they'd kill her. They could even have killed her as soon as she'd finished on the phone with me. I gambled that they'd check it out before they did that. Just to make sure I hadn't double-crossed them. The world they live in and the people they deal with are used to double crosses. I told the man who picked it up that I'd kept back part of the information and what I wanted in exchange for the rest. Hopefully he told Ruiz that when he handed it over. If they check it, they'll see that only some of the information is there. I offered the rest in exchange for Jenny.'

'And you think they'll buy that?' Maxwell asked.

'Maybe. Maybe not. They might decide to cut their losses and run. But it might buy us and her a little more time while they consider it. And if they do decide to make a run for it, at least they won't have got all the information on the flash drive.' Gawn hesitated before explaining, 'I phoned Takenaka while we were waiting to see if Jenny contacted me. He provided a USB with a built-in tracker. He's been following its location. That was him on the phone just now. We know where they are. Ruiz headed towards Newtownards. We've just got the map reference. That was what I gave Erin. The ARU were on standby at the airfield anyway so they can be there quickly.'

He had been surprised at her admission and he still didn't know if she meant Madson or Takenaka as the devil she'd done the deal with. He didn't care if it meant they could get Jenny back.

'What are we waiting for?' he asked.

This time he was out the door before her.

Chapter 65

Gawn was standing with Howard Vance from the armed response team. Both were dressed all in black. She had discarded her suit jacket and donned a black polo neck sweater and a set of body armour. A heavy belt encircled her waist holding all sorts of equipment, most importantly her Glock 17.

It was a long time since she had felt like this. The feeling just before an op begins; that mixture of excitement and fear and anticipation of the unknown. Being on the edge. Seb had told her she was an adrenaline junkie; that she got her highs from danger. She hadn't argued with him.

She glanced across to where Hill and Dee were standing together. She could see nervousness and anxiety on their faces. They hadn't been where she had been; hadn't experienced what she had experienced. They were frightened of what might happen. There was no harm in that. It would make them careful. Being frightened and going into danger anyway was bravery in her book, not the gung-ho attitude which risked your own life and others' too that she had seen sometimes in the past.

An OS map and some photographs were spread out on the bonnet of a police Land Rover and Vance was pointing out their position in relation to the target.

'This is us,' he said. 'They're here. The cottage isn't marked on the map. It must be a new build. I'm trying to get hold of the plans from the local council in case a siege develops. We managed to get a couple of aerial photos from the drone but I didn't want it overhead for too long in case they spotted it.'

'We want to take them here.' Gawn's voice displayed none of the tension she was feeling. 'We can't let this develop into a siege and we can't let it turn into a chase. They mustn't get as far as the airfield or into Newtownards, Howard.'

'Understood.'

Vance had started to fold the map up, when Gawn became aware of a commotion behind her and Takenaka came striding across to them. He was dressed more or less as he had been the first time she had walked into Reid's office and found him there. His suit with its razor-sharp creases, his crisp white shirt with button-down collar, the neatly knotted tie and the highly polished shoes all looked more appropriate for a business meeting rather than their present situation.

'I made it. Though your men didn't seem very keen to let me through.'

His voice was friendly but his eyes displayed something of his displeasure. This man was used to being in charge and used to getting his own way.

'They were just carrying out their orders, Agent Takenaka. We've secured the area. We don't want anyone just wandering in and getting caught up in all this.'

'So, how are you going to play it, Chief Inspector?' the American asked.

Gawn was suddenly aware of Vance and that the two men didn't know each other.

'This is Howard Vance. He's heading the ARU. This is Special Agent Takenaka of the FBI.'

'So, he's in charge then,' Takenaka said. 'I guess I should be asking him.' The American turned his gaze on the other man.

'This is *my* operation,' Gawn replied. 'Inspector Vance and his team are providing support if it's needed.'

Gawn wanted to make herself very clear. She wasn't going to let Takenaka or anyone else force her hand.

She glanced at her watch. It was nearly 6pm. Madson and her partner would need to be setting out soon for the airfield to make their take-off time. They'd be cutting it fine.

'So how are you going to play it?' Takenaka asked again and then folded his arms across his chest.

She recognised the body language. She'd seen it before from some of her male colleagues in the army. A challenge. Show me what you've got, your best shot, and I'll tell you what's wrong with it, it seemed to say.

'From the reconnaissance photos you can see the property is ringed by trees which makes it nice and private for Madson. It can't be seen from the road but it also gives us plenty of cover. We have people within fifteen feet of the building. We'll wait until they come out. They'll have to walk across this bit of open space to get to their car. As soon as they do we'll start to cut off their route back into the property; prevent it turning into a siege. If it's a choice between prison and being killed, I'm betting Madson'll choose prison and hope she can bargain her way to a lighter sentence. She knows a lot of things about a lot of people. She'll have bargaining power. Not so much here maybe but more so over your side of the pond.' She nodded to Takenaka. 'And I take it you'll be pushing for extradition. That might take years, meanwhile she'll be in the British system with no death penalty.'

'You've done your homework, Chief Inspector.'

And she had. She had gone over every piece of information she'd been able to get her hands on from sources she trusted about this woman's past career and criminal record. And she had called up favours from some of those mutual friends Takenaka had talked of. She was backing her own instincts about how Madson would react when they confronted her. She could be wrong and, if she was, it could cost Jenny Norris her life.

Chapter 66

Each minute seemed an hour. She must have glanced at her watch at least five times since they had all taken up their positions. Waiting was always the hardest part.

Then her phone rang.

'Yes … Yes, I know who you are.'

The men gathered around her listening. Maxwell, Vance and Takenaka stood silently.

'I have it … Yes, but I want to speak to Jenny Norris first … No, not unless I can speak to her and know she's alright … Then, when I see her, I'll hand it over to you.'

Maxwell watched Gawn's face. It broke into a smile of relief.

'Jenny, are you alright? … It's nearly over. Hold on … OK … Yes, I know the airfield … Fifteen minutes. I'll be there … Alone? … Yes. I understand.'

She looked up.

'I'm to bring the rest of the information to the airfield. I'm to go alone and they've only given me fifteen minutes to get there.'

'You know they plan to kill you and the hostage once they get the USB and then take off into the wild blue yonder?' Takenaka stated.

'Of course. But they're never going to get there, are they?'

Chapter 67

They had a view of the building on a long-range surveillance camera hidden in the trees and Gawn was watching a monitor showing what was happening. Suddenly there was a movement. She stiffened. The door opened and light spilled out into the clearing in front of the building. A man came out carrying two suitcases. It was Ruiz. She recognised him. He opened the boot of the BMW and placed the bags inside. Then he walked back to the bungalow. He wasn't being cautious. He obviously didn't expect any trouble and that was good for them. Surprise was their best weapon.

'Hold until I give the word.' Gawn spoke into the radio but her voice was barely above a whisper. They knew to wait anyway.

The door opened again. More slowly this time, it seemed, or maybe everything was going to happen in slow motion from now on. That was probably how she would remember it anyway. Jenny Norris, her hands tied in front of her, stumbled out catapulted forward by a push in the back. She was limping. Jenny's hair was hanging down over her face but Gawn could still see enough to recognise she had been beaten. At least she was able to walk, albeit haltingly and with support from Madson. The American was carrying a handbag and her other hand was clutching Jenny by the upper arm, directing her towards the car. So, no gun. She probably had one. Gawn was sure she did. In her handbag. But she didn't have it in her hand and that gave them an edge.

Now just for Ruiz to appear again. He needed to come out before Madson and Jenny reached the car otherwise there could be a standoff if Madson was able to shelter behind the vehicle with Jenny as a hostage. Gawn's hands were sweating. Her heart was racing. Each step nearer to the vehicle made it more likely this would end in shots fired.

And then, just like that, Ruiz reappeared. The door opened, he stepped out and didn't even bother closing the door behind him. He was carrying a box this time. Quite a big box. In both arms. She recognised the logo of Eureka Advances. This was their chance. It could all be over very soon.

'Now!'

Gawn shouted the command, not trying to disguise that something was going to happen, wanting the two Americans to hear, to not know who was coming at them and from where. A helicopter appeared overhead and spotlighted the three figures. Officers rushed forward out of the surrounding undergrowth, seeming almost to materialise as if by magic. There was a lot of shouting, the police identifying themselves and calls of, 'Get down! Down on the ground! Now!'

The Americans were surrounded by heavily armed men. Ruiz dropped the box and his hand moved to his jacket but he was grabbed from behind by a trio of burly officers who had appeared from round the back of the building and forced him to the ground, pinning him there while he was handcuffed.

Madson had made no move. She froze. She didn't try to run. She raised her hands in surrender as soon as all the commotion began and lay down on the ground with her hands behind her head when ordered to. Gawn watched as Jamie Grant knelt beside her and cuffed her hands behind her back. She saw his excited expression and knew he would be regaling his mates for weeks with his experiences of arresting an international criminal wanted by the FBI.

Gawn ran to Jenny Norris where she was lying on the ground in the middle of the clearing having obeyed the instruction to get down. Her hands, still tethered, were over her head trying to protect herself.

'Jenny. Jenny, are you OK?'

She knelt down beside her and turned her over gently. She helped her sit up and moved her hair back from her face. She couldn't help herself reacting to the bruises, the black eyes, one almost closed, and her lip swollen and encrusted with blood. She'd taken a hell of a beating. She threw her arms around her. Jenny seemed dazed. She still hadn't spoken.

'Where are you hurt?'

There was blood down the front of Jenny's shirt but it was old, dried in, and Gawn guessed it had probably come from the beating she had received. Gawn could barely hear her over the shouting all around them.

'I'm OK. I think. I…'

But she couldn't manage to say anything more and burst into tears and gulped for air between her sobs. Gawn put her arms around her and just hugged her and the pair rocked back and forth in the middle of the clearing. Paramedics arrived quickly and took over. Gawn was loath to let her go, holding her friend's hand as they put Jenny on a gurney and wheeled her to a waiting ambulance.

'Well done, Chief Inspector. A highly successful operation.'

Takenaka had walked up behind her where she was standing watching the ambulance drive off, lights flashing but no siren. The American was saying all the right words and yet Gawn realised he seemed disappointed. Had he wanted it to end in a shootout? Maybe save any problems with trying to extradite his two fugitives? It could take years of legal wrangles to sort out and the possibility of the press getting wind of what had really been going on.

'Successful for us and for the hostage, yes. Maybe not so much for you?'

'I don't know what you mean.'

He turned an exaggeratedly puzzled look in her direction. She took a flash drive from her pocket and handed it to him satisfied that she had logged the original into the evidence room back at headquarters.

'I think this is what you came for. Safe journey home, Agent Takenaka.' She turned and began to walk away.

Takenaka called after her and she turned to look at him as he spoke.

'Our mutual friends were right what they said about you. Until our paths cross again, Major Girvin.' He half-saluted her, then walked away.

Chapter 68

Gawn had slept well. She had been exhausted, after surviving on her nerves and coffee for days. This morning all the interviews and paperwork would start. It was not her favourite part of the job but it had to be done.

She was surprised when McKeown rushed out into the corridor as she passed the Serious Crimes office and stopped her.

'ACC Wilkinson's been on the phone, ma'am. She wants to see you. Right away.'

Gawn noted her sergeant's worried expression. Some of the younger woman's anxiety immediately transferred to her. She knew she had cut a lot of corners and bent a lot of rules in her search for her friend and maybe it was all catching up with her now. Ferguson might have put in an official complaint about her after all. If they had found drugs at Altor Pharmaceuticals, DCI Tomas O'Callaghan, newly appointed to lead the Anti-Drugs Initiative in Crime Operations could be knocking on the chief constable's door complaining that they hadn't been informed earlier of her suspicions. She could even be in trouble for talking to Miriam Florescu without making appropriate arrangements for a lawyer and translator, and then there was Hartnett. If Hughes had told his brief about her threats of extraordinary rendition to get him to talk she could definitely be in hot water.

She paused outside the ACC's door and waited a second to calm her churning stomach. Then she knocked.

'Come in.'

'Good morning, ma'am.' As Gawn greeted her boss trying to sound more confident than she felt, she looked past the seated woman to a man standing with his back to her. He was looking out the window his hands clasped behind his back. He turned round slowly and Gawn recognized him.

'You know Assistant Chief Constable Rennie,' Wilkinson said.

'Good morning, sir.' Gawn's voice didn't betray her surprise. She didn't know him, had never met him, but she knew of him. Of course, she should have expected he would be involved. He led the PSNI's Specialist Operations Branch dealing with national security.

Gawn braced herself for what was coming. She stood at attention, waiting to hear what was going to be said.

'This is a need-to-know briefing, Chief Inspector,' Rennie began, his voice serious, his words clipped, his stare unrelenting. 'Anything said in this room stays in this room. You cannot share it with any of your team or with Superintendent McDowell or CS Reid.'

'Yes, sir. I understand.'

'Your two suspects – Madson and Ruiz – have been handed over to our American colleagues.'

Gawn's face must have shown how she felt about that even though she had tried to conceal her reaction.

'They were a bit more than suspects, sir,' she began but Rennie held up his hand to stop her saying anything more.

'Be that as it may, they are gone. We were asked to cooperate with the American authorities on a matter of national security, both theirs and ours. A decision was taken at the highest level that it would be best for them to be returned to the US and questioned and dealt with there.'

'You mean offered a deal and witness protection in return for their testimony.'

Gawn was angry. She had been looking forward to being face to face with Emily Madson and being able to question her.

'What happens to them does not concern you.' Rennie's voice was cold. His eyes bored into her as he spoke. 'They will be dealt with appropriately.'

'But what about my murder case, sir?' Gawn asked.

'It's going to have to go down as unsolved,' Wilkinson said, her voice displaying some sympathy.

'That will affect your clear-up rate, but it can't be helped,' Rennie said. Gawn thought she detected a smugness in his expression.

'I'm not concerned about my bloody clear-up rate, sir. I'm concerned about a murderer walking free,' Gawn responded angrily.

She saw his eyes widen in surprise at her angry comment. Gawn realised she needed to keep calm. There was no point in antagonising Rennie. Whatever was done was out of her hands and his, she suspected.

'I think we can assume the two Americans will not get off lightly. Madson has been involved in arms dealing for years. The American authorities say the weapons she provided have already led to countless deaths across America and Europe, including here in Northern Ireland but this one was going to be the big payday. She had linked up with the Frate, as you know. They were already under surveillance by our European counterparts. The weapons this group were going to provide would have killed a lot of people. That won't happen now. The information on that USB along with Madson's testimony will allow them to round up some very dangerous men. There was even the possibility' – Rennie hesitated as if he wasn't sure how much he should say – 'of a threat to the national government from these militia groups if they had got hold of the arms. Balance that against a life sentence for murder here – if we could have got a conviction, which is by no means certain. She would probably have been out in a few years at most. There's no competition, is there?'

'What about Hughes?' Gawn asked.

'He didn't kill his wife, did he?' Wilkinson asked.

'No, ma'am. He admitted to fighting with her but not to killing her.'

'As far as our intel goes…and I questioned Hughes myself earlier this morning,' Rennie explained, 'he was just a pawn. He put his wife's DNA on a database and that started the whole ball rolling. Madson had a grudge about her background and her missing sister. But she'd already planned to come to Europe to meet with the Frate anyway. They were providing the weapons, she was arranging their transportation to America and negotiating their distribution. She learned about some financial difficulties that Altor was experiencing from Hughes, and so she asked the Frate to put pressure on Rodway to use the company's longstanding links to California to smuggle the guns, but then the Romanians got wind of the new drug and wanted a cut of it as well. They were after the USB and Madson needed to work with them over the weapons while hiding the USB from them. She gave it to Hughes for safe-keeping. He hid it with his wife and she passed it on to Dr Norris.'

'A very dangerous pass-the-parcel which made Dr Norris a target for both the Frate and Madson,' Wilkinson added.

'And Hughes knew nothing about it all?' Gawn asked.

'Nothing. He had grandiose ideas about finding some miracle drug or cure or something. He's a dreamer but not a gun runner or a murderer,' Rennie answered her question.

'And the whole story about Huntington's disease?'

'Just that, Chief Inspector. A handy story for Madson to spin to Hughes to get him worried that his wife could contract it. It allowed her to form a bond with him and then eventually to seduce him. From what I've learned about her, I'm sure she enjoyed stealing her sister's husband.'

'And a handy story for Takenaka to spin to explain his presence here,' Gawn finished his thoughts for him.

'Indeed, Chief Inspector,' Wilkinson agreed. 'It allowed Agent Takenaka to approach us officially but outside the remit of SOB or the Security Services,' she explained. 'So, as far as McDowell and Reid and your team are concerned, Madson and Ruiz were wanted for multiple counts of murder and it was decided that took precedence over a single murder charge here which we might or might not have been able to bring to court, so they were extradited. They didn't fight it. They went voluntarily. Not surprising. So they're already back on American soil. And Hughes won't be kicking up a fuss about his wife's killers getting away either. He'll be glad to cooperate with the American authorities.'

Gawn was sure he would be.

'You're being told this because you seem to have worked most if it out anyway. May I ask how, Chief Inspector?' Rennie asked.

'I know how the CIA works, sir. I've come across men like Takenaka before. I know how they operate and I know not to trust them,' she explained. 'I had my sergeant check the details of his story about Madson and Ruiz and it didn't stack up so I called in some favours from old colleagues, some of whom were or still are CIA.'

'I suppose I should say "Good work, Chief Inspector".'

Rennie might have been being sarcastic or maybe he really was impressed. She hoped she wasn't on his radar now. She preferred to deal with ordinary criminals.

'So now you know all we do,' Rennie stated.

Gawn doubted that. They would have told her as much as they felt they needed to. There was probably more but she didn't care. Harriet Hughes' murderer wouldn't escape justice. The Americans would use her and inevitably she would meet a sticky end. People like her who lived on the edge always did. And Jenny Norris was safe. She would recover physically and her reputation would be intact. Gawn could accept that.

Wilkinson cleared her throat before speaking.

'There has been a suggestion that you should have recused yourself from the investigation at the very beginning and of, shall we say, some unorthodox methods especially in a number of informal interviews of which there is no record, Chief Inspector. However, there will be no investigation by the Discipline and Anti-Corruption Branch as the whole case is now closed. Do we understand each other, Chief Inspector Girvin?' Wilkinson asked holding Gawn's gaze.

So, this was the quid pro quo. She said nothing and all her corner-cutting activities disappeared.

'Yes, ma'am. I understand.'

Epilogue

Maxwell and Gawn were sitting side by side on the edge of Jenny's sofa like a pair of schoolkids on their best behaviour visiting their granny while the pathologist was sunk down into a comfy armchair at the window, enjoying the low winter sunshine. A tartan rug was tucked in around her knees and her mother was fussing passing round cups of tea and coffee and a plate of scones.

'I'm going to go now, love.'

'You don't need to go because of us, Mrs Norris,' Gawn assured her.

'No. No. You're alright. I need to get home. I have to get Arnold's tea ready and then I have a Weight Watchers class tonight though you wouldn't think it the way I tucked into those scones when I was baking them this morning.'

The woman laughed and she rested her hand lightly on her daughter's shoulder.

'I'll be back first thing tomorrow, love.'

'Thanks, Mum.' Jenny reached across and put her hand on top of her mother's for just a second.

The trio didn't speak until Mrs Norris was safely out the door and it had closed firmly behind her. Maxwell was too busy anyway tucking into his second scone with jam and cream to add much to the conversation.

'Your mum's a brilliant baker,' he mumbled as he wiped a dab of cream off the side of his mouth.

'Yes. She is.' Jenny smiled. 'She likes you. But then she likes anyone who appreciates her baking.'

'What have the doctors said about time off?' Gawn asked. 'You shouldn't try to come back too soon, you know, Jenny.'

The pathologist already looked better than she'd expected. The bruises on her face had begun to fade a little; the areas around her eyes were less black but her eyes still looked haunted when Gawn looked into them. Her main injuries had been to her ankles where she had been shackled, and to her mind having endured days of threats and not knowing what was going to happen to her. Gawn knew all about PTSD. Jenny might think she was alright and she could just shrug it off and let life go back to normal but it wasn't that easy. She didn't know it yet, but life would never be normal again. Her own experiences still haunted Gawn sometimes.

'They're happy to leave it up to me. Anyhow I've decided I won't be rushing back. I'm going to give myself some time. Mum's talking about the two of us going on a wee cruise. It's something she's always wanted to do and Dad never had any interest. My sister could never go because of the children so it would be just the two of us. A good chance to catch up, make up for all the time we've lost. She fancies seeing the fjords.'

Gawn was delighted. She had phoned Helen Norris as soon as Jenny had been dispatched in the ambulance. She had hoped the woman would want to know her daughter was safe and was pleased when she asked which hospital and said she would meet them there.

'What was on that USB that made it worth killing for, Gawn? And what's going to happen now?' Jenny asked.

Gawn paused to consider how much she could say.

'Sorry,' Jenny said. 'I shouldn't have asked.'

'No. If anyone has a right to know, it's you.'

'I wouldn't mind hearing it too, Jenny. I think our friend here has been holding out on me.' Maxwell laughed but Gawn realised he was half-serious. She did feel a little guilty about keeping him in the dark.

'It turns out Madson was wanted for murder in several states. But as well there was a new formula for amphetamines on the USB. They would have been cheaper and easier to manufacture and more addictive meaning greater profits for the dealers. Information on all the deals she'd made for the drugs with details of where any handovers were going to take place with the dates and names were on the USB too.'

Gawn had cleared it with Wilkinson that she could tell her team and Jenny Norris about the drugs. It added more credence to why the two Americans had been so sought after and helped convince Maxwell not to ask too many awkward questions. No mention was to be made of the weapon smuggling.

'Hughes won't be charged for his attack on Harriet. We don't have enough evidence. Sorry,' Gawn said. 'The Americans will face murder and kidnapping charges. But you'll be kept out of it. You won't have to give evidence against them. You don't need to worry about that.'

'I can't help wondering if I'd never encouraged Harri to leave Edward whether any of this would have happened.'

'You can't think like that, Jenny. None of us can second-guess ourselves. We can only do our best. It wasn't your fault. Madson chose to use her visit to Europe to settle her own private score. Hughes would still have contacted her because he wanted information for his so-called research which was just some pipe dream of winning a Nobel prize. Truth be told, he's not really much of a geneticist. Altor only kept him on because of Harriet's money.

'And Madson would still have wanted to get her revenge on her sister. And once he chose to start an affair with her, he sealed Harriet's fate. No matter if she'd still been living with Edward, Madson would have wanted her dead. She's a very twisted, wicked woman who hated a sister she'd never even met. She's screwed up.'

Maxwell had sat silently eating the last scone as she was explaining all this to her friend. Now he piped up.

'Gawn has so many brownie points with the bosses at the minute, it's unreal. Not only did she best the FBI but she even managed to tip off the Drugs Squad about something fishy going on at Altor, and when they raided it they found a whole smuggling set-up they knew nothing about.'

The three had finished their afternoon tea and Maxwell was dispatched to tidy the dishes away.

'There have to be some perks to rank, Paul, and being the brass's flavour of the month,' Gawn joked as he carried the plates and cups into the kitchen area and rolled up his sleeves ready to wash and stack them.

She wanted a quiet word with Jenny alone but it was the pathologist who spoke first.

'Before you say anything, I want to thank you, Gawn. I haven't had a chance to do that properly. I knew they'd ditched old Betsey in Strangford Lough, you see. I was half-conscious but I saw Ruiz pushing her into the water. I worked out that everyone was supposed to think I'd committed suicide but I just knew you'd still be looking for me. Thank you for not giving up.'

'Well, I'm that crazy bitch who's mad enough to do anything, haven't you heard?' Gawn laughed.

'Harri didn't deserve what happened to her, you know, Gawn. There was nothing between us. I'd have told you if there was but I'll miss our walks in the Mournes. She was a good friend and a good person. Maybe, in time, it could have been something more. I'll never know now.'

Gawn reached across and patted her friend's hand. Then she continued, almost shyly, changing the subject, 'I'm going over to the States to see Seb the day after tomorrow. Reid has signed off on a few extra days' leave for me. Thanks to my brownie points as Paul calls it. I'll only be there for five days but it'll keep us going until I see him at Christmas.'

'That's great. I'm sure he's delighted.'

'He's over the moon. But I have some good news for him as well. I didn't want to have to tell him over the phone.' Gawn smiled and Jenny knew what she was going to say. 'I got the results back from Dublin. They say there's no reason I can't get pregnant. Everything's still in reasonably good working order apparently. It's just with the scarring and my age, it reduces my chances but it can still happen.'

'Right, dishes duty done, ma'am.' Maxwell strode back over to the two women and mock-saluted Gawn as he picked his jacket up from the back of the sofa. 'Kerri has me well trained, you know. Cheerio, Jenny. Good to see you looking so well. Take care of yourself. See you soon but not too soon, eh? Enjoy your cruise and send us a postcard.' He bent over and gave her a friendly peck on the cheek.

'Bye, Jen,' Gawn said. The two women hugged. 'I'll see you when I get back.'

'Don't bother packing too many clothes for your trip, Gawn. I don't expect you'll need them,' Jenny called after them and laughed suggestively.

Maxwell gave his boss a funny look.

'What was that about? Oh, I suppose you'll be spending all your time on the beach.'

'Yes, something like that, Paul.' And Gawn laughed too.

If you enjoyed this book, please let others know by leaving a quick review on Amazon. Also, if you spot anything untoward in the paperback, get in touch. We strive for the best quality and appreciate reader feedback.

editor@thebookfolks.com

MORE IN THIS SERIES

THE PERFUME KILLER (Book 1)

Stumped in a multiple murder investigation, with the only clue being a perfume bottle top left at a crime scene, DCI Gawn Girvin must wait for a serial killer to make a wrong move. Unless she puts herself in the firing line…

MURDER SKY HIGH (Book 2)

When a plane passenger fails to reach his destination alive, Belfast police detective Gawn Girvin is tasked with understanding how he died. But determining who killed him begs the bigger question of why, and answering this leads the police to a dangerous encounter with a deadly foe.

A FORCE TO BE RECKONED WITH (Book 3)

Investigating a cold case about a missing person, DCI Gawn Girvin stumbles upon another unsolved crime. A murder. But that is just the start of her problems. The clues point to powerful people who will stop at nothing to protect themselves, and some look like they're dangerously close to home.

KILLING THE VIBE (Book 4)

After a man's body is found with strange markings on his back, DCI Girvin and her team try to establish his identity. Convinced they are dealing with a personally motivated crime, the trail leads them to a group of people involved in a pop band during their youth. Will the killer face the music or get off scot-free?

MURDER ON THE TABLE (Book 6)

A charity dinner event should be a light-hearted affair, but two people dying as the result of one is certainly likely to put a damper on proceedings. DCI Gawn Girvin is actually an attendee, and ready at the scene to help establish if murder was on the table. But the bigger question is why, and if Gawn can catch a wily killer.

NOTHING BUT SMILES (Book 7)

A serial stalker is terrorising women on the streets of Belfast. The victims wake up with no recollection of the night before, but with a smiley-face calling card daubed on their bodies. DCI Gawn Girvin takes on the case although before long she herself is targeted. She must catch the sick creep before matters escalate.

OTHER TITLES OF INTEREST

THE GIRL IN THE MEADOW by John Dean

When the body of a young woman is discovered under the floorboards of an isolated house during its renovation, questions are raised about DCI Jack Harris' own potential connection to the site. Will he clear his name or will his reputation be forever besmirched in the rural Pennine community?

WHERE WOLVES PROWL by James Andrew

When loner Jason is invited by an attractive girl to a luxury private pool party on Nairn's seafront, he can't quite believe his luck. But when he learns the next day that someone was murdered during the event, things take a turn for the worse. As an outsider, he falls under suspicion. Can he find out who the killer is and prove his innocence?

Printed in Great Britain
by Amazon

40596557R00138